I don't know why I got cancer, and don't think I haven't asked! The doctors don't know, Mom and Dad don't know. Maybe it's just bad luck. But whatever it is, I sure do hate it. This doesn't seem real. I keep thinking this is a bad dream and I'll wake up any minute. But I don't wake up. And I have to take chemo treatments, which scare me to death. Gee, did I really mean to write "death"? Oh, Jesse, I wish I could see you. . . . I wish this wasn't happening to me. . . . I just want to go home and have everything the way it used to be.

Lurlene McDaniel

A Rose
for Melinda

LAUREL-LEAF BOOKS

Published by
Dell Laurel-Leaf
an imprint of
Random House Children's Books
a division of Random House, Inc.
New York

Visit us on the Web! www.randomhouse.com/teens

**Educators and librarians, for a variety of teaching tools,
visit us at www.randomhouse.com/teachers**

ISBN: 0-553-57090-0

RL: 4.7

Printed in the United States of America

A Bantam Book/August 2002
First Laurel-Leaf edition March 2004

10 9 8 7 6

OPM

This book is dedicated to
Trevor Clark McDaniel, a lamb of God.

My deep appreciation to Dr. Mary Duffy—
thanks for sharing your expertise!

Blossoms

WELCOME TO MRS. BARBER'S
1ST-GRADE CLASS
ROOM 105, BEN FRANKLIN
ELEMENTARY SCHOOL

RULES:

1. Raise your hand to ask a question.

2. Take turns.

3. No hitting, no shoving, no talking.

4. Bring notebook to school every day.

5. Be kind to each other.

September 7

Dear Melinda Skye,
   Thank you for sharing your snack.
You are very pretty.

Signed,
your friend,
Jesse Rose

September 7

Dear Jesse Rose,
   Thank you. I have new shoes. Do you
like them?

Your friend,
Melinda Skye

October 1

Dear Melinda,
   I don't like school. But I like you.
Do you like me?

Your friend,
Jesse

October 1

Dear Jesse,
   I like you. But I like school. Reading is
the best part.

Your friend,
Melinda

October 2

Dear Melinda,
  The best part of school is seeing you.

Your very good friend,
Jesse

P.S. I like baseball. I want to play for the Braves. They are my favorite team.

October 3

Dear Jesse,
  I like ballet. I take classes and want to be a real ballerina. I will be famous.

Your friend,
Melinda

October 21

Dear Mr. and Mrs. Rose,

I'm afraid that Jesse must be placed on an "in-room" suspension from recess for the next three days for fighting on the playground. Although he has assured me that he "only socked Toby Gillman in the nose because he shoved Melinda Skye off the swing," as his teacher, I can't allow physical attacks on fellow students to occur. Please understand that I think Jesse is a good child. He has never disrupted the class until this unfortunate incident. As you are aware, this school system has a zero-tolerance policy regarding physical violence, and therefore Jesse must be punished for his aggressive act toward another student. Please call our principal if you have any questions regarding Jesse's suspension. Be assured that Toby is receiving the same punishment for shoving Melinda.

Sincerely,
Nancy Barber

October 22

Mrs. Barber,

Jesse has told his father and me that he will not hit Toby again "UNLESS Toby hurts Melinda." We've always tried to instill a sense of right and wrong in our son, and he knows that hitting others is wrong. For some reason, Jesse has formed an attachment to Melinda and feels a need to defend her—like some kind of mini-Lancelot. We understand and accept his punishment and are confident that he will behave in the future if Toby behaves.

Sincerely,
Ann Rose

Dear Jesse,

Thank you for punching Toby for me. I am sorry you have to miss recess, but I will sit with you at lunch all next week because you are my hero.

Friends forever,
Melinda

December 4

Dear Melinda,
   I made this picture for you. It's me playing baseball and you watching. Do you like it?

Jesse

December 5

Dear Jesse,
   I like the picture a lot!!!!! I put it in my room.

Melinda

An Invitation
To: Jesse Rose
From: Melinda Skye
Date: December 16, Friday
Time: 7:30 P.M.
Place: Memorial Auditorium

Jesse—Melinda wants you to come watch her dance in the "Nutcracker Suite" next weekend. She is one of the cherubs in the dance company and will be in the front row. Perhaps your parents will bring you, and after the performance, you can all come backstage and say hello.

Elana Skye (Melinda's mom)

[Transcript from the VCR of Leonard and Elana Skye. Scene of backstage bedlam as girls dressed in tutus and leotards scurry around shrieking and giggling.]

OFF-CAMERA VOICE OF LEONARD SKYE: Slow down, Princess. There's somebody here to see you.

[Camera swings around to show Jesse and his parents. Jesse walks over to Melinda, hands her a pink rose wrapped in tissue.]
JESSE: I liked . . . I mean, you danced real good. I stayed awake the whole time!

MELINDA *[giggles]:* A rose? For me? *[Glances up at camera]* Look, Daddy, Jesse brought me a rose. A rose from a Rose. *[Giggles again]*

ELANA *[Steps into camera shot, bends down]*: This is just beautiful. How thoughtful, Jesse. *[Looks up]* Thank you for bringing him.

[Camera swings and shot widens to include Jesse's smiling parents.]
ANN ROSE: He saw that on television . . . you know, the part about giving an actress, or dancer in this case, a bouquet of roses after the final curtain. He insisted he bring roses for Melinda.

JOHN ROSE: I took him to the florist and he bought it with his own money.

VOICE OF JESSE: That's why there's just one. They cost a whole lot!

[Camera swings around and zooms in on Jesse's face as all adults laugh off-camera.]
ELANA: What do you say to Jesse, honey?

MELINDA: Thank you a whole bunch. *[Throws arms around Jesse and kisses him wetly on the cheek. Adults laugh. Jesse's eyes widen. Camera pulls back and kids wave at lens.]*

[Fade to Black]

Memo
To: All Parents
From: Nancy Barber
Date: May 20

To commemorate the end of the school year, we will hold a small "graduation" ceremony on Friday, the last day of classes. All family members are invited to this ceremony, which will be held at 3 P.M. in the cafeteria. Please plan to attend if at all possible. I am proud of each student and want everyone to have a sense of a job well done!

Report cards will go out within two weeks of the end of classes. Have a wonderful summer!

May 23

Dear Melinda,
I will miss you very much all summer. I will write to you, OK? My mom said it is all right with her if your mom says I can. Will you miss me too?

Jesse

P.S. Can I be your boyfriend? Like a REAL boyfriend, not just a boy who is a friend?

May 23

Dear Jesse,

Yes, I will miss you. Yes, let's write. I am going to dance camp in July. I am going to visit my Grandma in Florida in August. I love her bunches and bunches. See you next year!

Melinda

P.S. My mom says I have to wait longer before I can have a real boyfriend. But thank you for asking.

P.P.S. If I could have a boyfriend, I would pick you!

Dear Mr. and Mrs. Skye,

Melinda has been a pleasure as a student. She's bright and outgoing with a delightful sunny disposition. Her love of reading and writing points to her being a stellar student with great success in the classroom. She is well able to express herself in writing, and if her dream of being a dancer doesn't *pan out, I think she'll make a wonderful writer someday!*

Sincerely,
Nancy Barber

Dear Mr. and Mrs. Rose,

Jesse is a kind and thoughtful boy with a big heart and a well-honed sense of caring. His test scores indicate that he's a very capable student, and I expect him to do well in the remainder of his school years. Although he can sometimes be shy and reserved, he knows what he wants and works hard to achieve his goals. I must say, he certainly has note-passing down to a science!

Sincerely,
Nancy Barber

June 12

Dear Elana,

Since school ended, Jesse has been bugging me to invite Melinda over so they can play. He says he misses her and doesn't want to wait until school starts before *he sees her again. Can I pick her up Wednesday morning? Or, if you'd like, come for coffee around ten, and we'll have a visit while they play. I so enjoyed your company in our shared room-mother duties last year and would like to catch up and talk about next year. Some changes are in the wind for the Rose family.*

Ann

——————— ❧ ———————

June 15

Dear Ann,

After our visit and talk the other day, I strongly wanted to write you some words of encouragement. Also, it's so difficult to talk with the kids hanging around, and as you said, you really don't want Jesse to know what's going on just yet.

First of all, every marriage has problems, so don't think that the situation between you and John is hopeless. I'm glad you've found a good counselor. Perhaps, in time, John will join you in therapy. Few problems get solved unless a couple works hard on them together.

Your getting a job when school starts seems like a good idea. I know it isn't easy to return to the workforce when you feel "underqualified and undereducated," but as you noted, we don't always get to do what we want.

Jesse is bright and so very nice. He'll weather the change. And Lenny and I will be circumspect about you and John around Melinda so that she doesn't ask Jesse questions he can't answer.

Remember, I'm here for you. Lenny and I will help however we can.

Elana

August 10

Dear Jesse,

Today we went to Walt Disney World. It's really fun, but I wish you were here to go on the rides with me. You'd like my grandma too. She's been sick, but she is feeling better now. Please don't be too worried about your mom and dad.

Parents argue. It's normal. I'll be home before school starts.

Melinda

You're Invited!!!!

Who: Melinda Skye, age 8
What: A Birthday Party
When: August 31, 3:00 P.M.
Where: Melinda's house

(Jesse, please come to my party because you are my best friend.)

Dear Jesse,
   The music box you gave me is my favorite thing. Thank you a whole bunch. I know it must be tough, but don't let Toby tease you about coming to my house after school now that your mom is at work. I know it isn't much fun for you when I have dance class, but that's only three days a week. The

other days we have lots to do. I'll get better at Nintendo. Maybe even beat you someday! Your idea of building a tree house is great. My dad said he would help us. And he will, too, because he always keeps his promises.

Melinda

September 12

Thank you for the baseball cards for my birthday. I did not invite you to a party, because I did not have one. Life is not very happy around my house. Coming to your house after school is great for me because it's fun. I am glad we are still best friends. I wish my mom and dad were happy like your mom and dad. You made my birthday a good one anyway. Thanks, Melinda.

Jesse

Greetings from the Atlanta Skyes!

Another year finds us all well and happy.
We'll begin with Lenny, who continues to
earn seniority at America South Air Lines
and rack up the miles as a pilot. We can't
believe he's flown the equivalent of twice
around the earth in the few years he's been
with the airline. For fun, he continues to
terrorize local golfers with his formidable
swing, and he says that his goal in life is
to play every major course in the states
before he's fifty. (Golfers of America, you
have been warned!)

I continue to chase after Melinda, who
keeps me on the go with her ballet classes
and school projects. Between helping sew
costumes at the dance studio and running
publicity for the upcoming presentation of
The Nutcracker (in which Melinda will
dance in the corps), I haven't had time to
catch my breath this fall. I also chaired
the autumn auction and fund-raiser for the
local children's hospital. I'm pleased to
say we met our goal! In fact, they've asked
me to chair the event again next year, and
of course I said yes.

As for Melinda, she's loving school, dance and more dance. We never dreamed she'd stick with it the way she has, but she's been fanatical about becoming a ballerina since she was five, so what can we do except support her?

My mom, in Florida, continues to decline in health, but she won't move into a care facility no matter how much I beg. She says, "I don't want to live in one of those. They're full of old people."

Sure hope this finds all our friends and family happy and healthy and ready to take on the New Year. Peace on Earth!

The Skyes

March 12

Dear Jesse,

I am very sorry you fell out of the tree house and broke your arm. Mom says that we can't play Batman and Batgirl up in the tree anymore. I guess we should have waited for my dad to tie the rope on the branch, because our knot wasn't a good one. My mom will make you good lunches while you stay at my house so your mother can go to work, and I'll bring your homework every day until you can come back to school. I think your cast is kind of neat. Thanks for letting me be the first to sign it. Please don't let Toby sign it. He's mean.

Melinda, your (Bat) friend

Elana and Lenny,

How can I thank you enough for all the help you've given me this school year? I wouldn't have made it without you, and neither would Jesse. He talks about Melinda and both of you constantly. You are so kind to include him in your family outings. And your offer to let him spend the summer at your house while I work is overwhelmingly generous. With my family way out in California, and John's in New York, I really don't have anyone to watch my son, and a day care center isn't where he wants to be.

As you know, John and I are separating. I'm not sure what I'll do when third grade begins in the fall,

*but something will work out one way or another. I feel
blessed that you are so generous and kind to us.*

As ever,
Ann

November 2

Dear Grandma,
   Third grade is fun. Lots more
homework, but I like my new teacher.
My friend Jesse and I are in different
classrooms this year, but he still comes
over after school and we do our
homework together. Guess what? Jesse
now can sleep over when his mom goes
out of town, because Mom fixed up
the room in the basement. Jesse's mom
went to California this week, so
Jesse's staying with us, and it's fun to
do homework and go to school
together. He's better than a brother,
I'm sure.
   Here's really good news! Mrs. Houston
picked ME to dance the part of Clara
in The Nutcracker this year. You know

how much I love to dance. Someday I will be a famous ballerina, so stay healthy so you can come see me when I get to dance on the great stage.

For Halloween, me and Jesse dressed up like Frankenstein (Jesse) and Miss Piggy (me). Mom stuffed my leotard with foam padding and Dad made a pig snout for me. Mom took pictures and said she'll send some to you. Jesse and I cleaned up in the candy department. We got a ton. But don't worry, I won't eat it all (at once . . . ha-ha). Did a lot of kids knock on your door? I still like little bags of chocolate kisses best.

Well, I guess that's it for now. I'll write again real soon.

XXXOOO
Melinda

P.S. I LOVE the diary you gave me for my birthday, and I write in it every night. When I've filled it up, I'm getting another one! It feels great to write down my feelings.

Seasons Greetings

Dear friends and family,

It's hard to begin a holiday letter on a sad note, but I must. After eleven years of marriage, John and I have agreed to split. This has not been an easy decision for either of us, but it is a necessary one.

Our house is on the market, and over the holidays Jesse and I will be moving to Santa Cruz, where we will live in the house I grew up in. I'm so glad I didn't sell it after my dad died last year. It should be a good place to resettle, and I have plans for us once we're there. I will work and also attend college so I can earn credits toward a degree in education. John has already moved out. He's taken a position with a company in New York.

Our new address is on the envelope of this letter and on the enclosed sheet. Our e-mail address remains the same. Please keep us in your thoughts. I must admit, Jesse is having a very hard time with all of this. But what child wouldn't? Maybe next year life will look brighter for us.

We still send our best wishes for a happy holiday!

Ann and Jesse

TO: Ballerina Girl
Subject: New Home

I am in California, but I don't like it here. I miss my dad. I miss my old friends, I miss my house, and most of all, I miss you and your mom and dad. I don't like my new school, and I have to go to an after-school program now. I don't like that either. I think about the fun we used to have, my special room at your house, and how great you and your parents were to me. I feel so lucky because I have those memories. I wish things were the way they used to be. I hope you will e-mail me A LOT!

How are things for you? How's school? When you are a famous ballerina, please don't forget me. Please.

Jesse

——————— ∿ ———————

Name: *Melinda Skye*
Date: *September 10*
Mrs. Garner, 6ᵗʰ grade

What I Did on My Summer Vacation

This summer was a dream come true! I went to dance camp in Tampa for two whole weeks! My ballet instructor in Atlanta, Mrs. Houston, learned that prima ballerina Petrina Milicoff, who once danced with the Bolshoi Ballet in Moscow, was offering summer classes to promising students. Mrs. Houston recommended me! My mother sent in my application plus a videotape of me performing. I received a letter of acceptance in June, right after school was out. I was so excited that I didn't sleep for days.

When the date finally arrived, Mom and I flew to Tampa, where I spent the hardest (and best!) two weeks of my life in a dance studio with Ms. Milicoff. Twenty-five girls were invited. Only three of us were twelve years old. Ms. Milicoff said I have "the look of a dancer" (which is not too tall or too short, long neck, long legs, and small bones). She encouraged me to continue my training in Atlanta and said that when I turn sixteen, I should try out for the corps of a troupe that travels to Europe during the summers. Sixteen seems like a long way off when I want something as much as I want this!

The other thing that happened this summer is I made a new friend. In August, the house across the street was sold (it's been empty for ages!) and Bailey Taylor—who is exactly my age (her birthday's July fourth!)—moved in with her parents, her twin half sisters (six years old), a dog and two cats. When I found out she was coming to Rosswell Middle School, I promised to be her friend. Bailey doesn't dance; she plays the flute (but she hates to practice). She reads tons of teen magazines and knows all the latest fashion news.

That's most of what happened to me over the summer. It's changed me some. If possible, I want to be a ballerina more than ever.

Melinda,

I'm in boring English and decided to write to you instead of taking boring English notes. I mean, who wants to know about Louisa May Alcott and her boring book? Besides, I already read one of her books at my school in Virginia. When we walk home today, let's stop off at the Jiffy Store and buy some teen magazines so we can figure out what's hot this fall. I have five dollars that I got for baby-sitting my bratty sisters.

Oh, before I forget, do you know Richie Manetta? He keeps staring at me and I don't want to let him know it matters. Unless, of course, he's really cool. Then I want to let him know it matters. But if he's totally a brick I will ignore him. Your word is the law!

Bailey

MELINDA'S DIARY

November 16

All Bailey talks about is getting a boyfriend. She asked me if I've ever had one and I told her I have a friend boy—a best friend who moved away but keeps in touch. That's Jesse, of course! He's not a boyfriend in the romantic sense. At least not for me. (He still sends me birthday and Christmas cards *from California.) OK, so maybe I'm being a little dishonest, but Bailey asked a hundred questions, so I dug out my memory box and showed her pictures of him. (Good thing he sent his school picture this year!)*

Bailey said he is really cute (which he is, but I never thought about it). And then she started pumping me about whether I'd ever kissed him and stuff like that. I told her I didn't want to get too personal, but she was like a dog with a bone and told me all about the boys she's kissed and blah-blah-blah. More information than I wanted. But it has made me think about being kissed. I wonder what it feels like? And as long as I'm thinking about it, I guess I'd rather kiss Jesse than any of the guys at school. Not that I'll probably ever see him again. Still, it's fun to think about. . . .

Not that I have time for a boyfriend. Ballet and school take up almost every minute of my life . . . except for the small part Bailey takes up asking dumb questions!

Hi and Merry Christmas!
Thanks for the photos you sent on the Web. You look really pretty in your ballet dress, and I know you must have danced really great in The Nutcracker this year. I still remember the time I

went backstage when we were in first grade. I thought you were pretty then too. I hope you remember.

I'm into skateboarding big-time and I'm in a competition in March, so I'm doing a lot of practicing at a park near my house where all us boarders hang. Mom's still in school and working. The other big news is that my dad remarried and now I have two stepbrothers. Dad wants me to visit them this summer in New York. I don't really want to go, but I'll have to. He tries to keep in touch, but now that he has a new family the divorce seems even harder on Mom.

I'll send you postcards from the city. Maybe we can e-mail each other too while I'm there. I know you'll probably be going to some dance school this summer, but I still think about the fun we had when we were kids. I sort of miss it. You have the best family and I used to wish my dad was more like yours. Instead, I have a dad that's like mine.

Your e-mails to me make me feel good. Have a good holiday and give a special hi to your great parents. Mom may take me up to the mountains to ski for a Christmas present!

Jesse

February 21

Jesse,

We had to make an emergency trip to Florida because my grandma is dying. I'm freaked. I really love her and I can't imagine never seeing her again. I'm so sad. So sad.

─────────────────────────────────

This is in two parts because Grandma died yesterday. The funeral is the day after tomorrow. I can't stop crying. More later.

Melinda

To all your family,

Jesse and I are so sorry about the loss of Melinda's grandmother and your mother, Elana. We both send our love.

With sympathy, Ann and Jesse Rose

Hi friend,

I'm so glad you're home from Florida and I'm so sorry about your grandmother. I was almost five when my grandpa died, but I remember it like it was yesterday.

Mom and Dad had just divorced and Dad had dropped out of our lives (whereabouts still unknown). Mom cried a lot. I was scared because I thought she might die too and then who was going to take care of me? Instead, she married Bill and had Brenda and Paula and talked about how much Grandpa would have loved seeing them and how they'd grow up and never get to know him. Which hurt my feelings because she never once mentioned how much he liked ME, or how much fun Grandpa and I used to have together.

Well, I didn't mean to go on about myself. Here's some happy news: My cat Bubbles is going to have kittens. Do you think your parents will let you have one? If so, you can pick out any one of the litter you want. Sort of in memory of your grandma.

Bailey

Bailey!
    Mom said I can have the kitten! And I will always love her and take care of her. You are a true friend!

Melinda

MELINDA'S DIARY

April 4

I love my kitten! She's pure white except for a black mask around her eyes, like Zorro. Jesse tells me I should name her Zorita because she's a female. Zorita sounds pu-r-r-rfect, so that's her name.

<Melinda> How are you, Jesse?

<Jesse> I'm fine. How's Zorita?

<Melinda> Cute as ever. There's somebody here I want you to meet.

<Bailey> Hi, Jesse. This is Bailey. I'm over at Melinda's house and we're IM'ing you together.

<Jesse> Hi, Bailey. Melinda says you play the flute.

<Bailey> That makes me sound so nerdy, and I'm not. I'm a real babe!

<Melinda> Yes, she's Bailey the Babe. All the guys at school think so. Ouch! Bailey just slugged my arm for telling you she's popular with the boys.

<Jesse> Don't slug Melinda! I'll be forced to polish you off like I did Toby Gillman. That's a story you can ask Melinda to tell you sometime.

<Bailey> Who's Toby? Someone tell me!

<Melinda> I just told her he was my tormentor in first grade. Now she's really impressed because you defended me. You were my hero!

<Jesse> That was then. What about now?

<Melinda> You still are!

<Bailey> Oh p-u-l-ease! I know

**when I'm being shut out. Nice
to meet you J. Adios.**

**<Melinda> Write me when you
get back from New York. Okay?
I'll keep my fingers crossed that
you like your "new" family.**

<Jesse> I hope so too. . . . Bye.

TO: Ballerina Girl
Subject: My New York Trip

The visit is over and I'm glad to be home. Because NY could never be home for me. The first week was awkward, everyone being extra polite and all. My stepbrothers, Richie and Darrin, didn't know how to treat me. They played games on their computer until Dad chewed them out for ignoring me. Neither one is very athletic. Dad got all over them, but it didn't make them want to hang with me at all. If we did do something together, it was just to be polite. His new wife, Donna, was nice to me, but she works, so she was not there during the day much.

Dad took ten days off work and we took trips into the city and out to some woods for hiking. That was okay. Sight-seeing highlights included the top of the Empire State Building, the ferry to Staten Island and the Statue of Liberty. One day Dad took us all to Yankee Stadium for a ball game, but it rained! We sat around for an hour waiting for it to clear up.

Truth is, Dad and I don't have much to talk about. We're strangers. That really hurts. When he put me on the plane home, we just stood there looking at each other. He said, "If you ever want to spend a summer here, just say the word." I know he wanted me to hug him, but I didn't want to. So I just said thanks and got on the plane. When I was younger, I used to dream about him begging me to come live with him and I would say no, hoping to hurt his feelings real bad. I still feel he shouldn't have left me and Mom. He shouldn't have. Your parents are so perfect. Maybe this is hard for you to under-stand—but thanks for being there to let me get it off my chest.

Jesse

TO: Ballerina Girl
Subject: Happy Birthday to my most Beloved Daughter!!!!

Sorry I must be away on your actual B-day, Princess, but I promise to make it up to you when I return. Paris is a beautiful city and I really want to bring you and Mom here for vacation. You'd love it! Of course, you usually find some ballet school to run off to during the summers, but maybe you can work in some vacation time with your parents. What do you think? There's a ballet to attend here and I'd be sure we'd get tickets.

I'll see you the day after tomorrow, so think about where you'd like to go for your birthday. Ask Mom for ideas too. You're thirteen! I can hardly believe it. I'm the father of a teenager! Love to my two favorite women!

Dad

MELINDA'S DIARY

September 6

School's barely started and I've already got a pile of homework—ugh! I wrote a long e-mail to Jesse trying to encourage him about his family troubles. It must be hard. He feels torn between his parents, but of course, he's really devoted to his mom. I wish I could see Jesse again, up close and personal. I really like him, but falling for someone who lives across the country doesn't make sense. Wish I were like Bailey and could find someone at school, but no one interests me the way Jesse does. Maybe someday, some boy will. Until then, Jesse is the one! I can't believe I've known him so long and we're still close. What or who could break that tie up?

❧

Atlanta School of Ballet

April 7

Atlanta School of Ballet
4325 Peachtree Blvd.
Atlanta, GA 30021

Dear Ms. Skye:

We are pleased to confirm your acceptance by the Washington School of Classical Dance for its summer training program, beginning June 14. This opportunity, offered only to approximately one hundred dancers in the country, will require you to live in the dorms and attend classes three times a day, six days a week. A packet from the Washington School will arrive shortly with all data pertaining to your scholarship. Once again, congratulations, and we look forward to your return to our school in the fall.

Sincerely,
Madeline Houston
Director

P.S. Melinda . . . we're so proud of your accomplishments. I can't think of a more deserving student than you. Congratulations! M.H.

MELINDA'S DIARY

April 8

I made it!!!! I can't believe it, but the letter came today confirming my acceptance into the best classical-dance training program in the whole country!!! Mom and I shouted and screeched and danced all around the kitchen when I read the letter to her.

In June, Mom and I fly up to Washington, D.C. Then Mom comes home and I stay up there two whole months doing the hardest, most disciplined work of my life! I'm excited, but scared too. I'll miss seeing Bailey every day. I'll miss Zorita's soft purr. I'll miss e-mailing Jesse. The competition will be fierce, but I've always wanted this.

I know that getting into the corps of a good ballet troupe is so very competitive that some of the girls would push you down a flight of stairs if they thought it might eliminate competition and better their chances. (What I just wrote sounds hateful, but it's the gospel truth!) Gosh, I hope I don't make any enemies.

Stop it, Melinda!!! (Sometimes I have to be stern with myself.) Just go and dance and learn!

"Hello, Melinda. It's me, Jesse."

"No way!"

"Way."

"You're calling me? From California? Is—is everything all right?"

"Of course. When I got your e-mail about being accepted into the Washington program, I asked Mom if I could call you and she said I could, so here I am."

"Oh, Jesse . . . this is so sweet of you. Really. I—I haven't heard your voice in years."

"How do I sound?"

"Great."

"You too. I'm kicked about your getting picked. I mean, I know how much you love ballet."

"But it's going to be hard, Jesse. I mean this is a whole different level."

"You scared?"

"A little."

"You're going to be the best."

"I just hope I don't embarrass myself. Some of the girls are sixteen and seventeen and ready to go off to real dance troupes. Dance masters come to watch us and pick the best and dismiss the others. Imagine, training all your life only to be told you're not 'suitable.' It's a crusher."

"That won't happen to you, Melinda. When you're sixteen, they'll fight over who'll get you."

"I hope! But enough about me. What about you, Jesse? Are you going to New York to see your father again this summer?"

"I can't get out of it."

"Promise me you'll give them another chance, OK?"

"I'll give them another chance. Um . . . Mom's making signs at me to hang up, so I've got to go."

"Thanks for calling. It means a lot to me."

"Write me from Washington. If you have the time, I mean."

"I'll find the time. Goodbye, Jesse."

"Bye. You know what? I miss you . . . even after all these years."

June 23

Dear Melinda,

I miss you like crazy! But I know you're loving it. Boy, from your letter, it sure sounds like you're really working hard. I can't believe you're not feeling good. What a pain to be up there competing with all those prima donnas and not feeling good.

Listen, I'm gonna bust if I don't tell you something. I was saving it till you got home, but I can't wait another minute. Here goes. I went to the mall last Friday and ran into Peter Keating. (Remember, I had a thing for him in September, but he was in high school and my parents squashed it.) Anyway, Pete asked me to go to the movie playing at the mall and I said "Sure." Inside it was practically empty and the theater was totally dark, and then Pete slid his arm around me and the next thing I knew he was KISSING me! Wow, I thought my nail polish would melt. It was SO hot! (And I don't mean the temperature.)

So now Pete and I are "on" again and he's coming over this Saturday while I baby-sit the twins and Mom and Bill go shopping. My plan is to lose the twins (temporarily) and practice kissing Pete. Gotta run now. More after Saturday!

Hugs,
Bailey

P.S. Sure wish you were going to be here for my birthday!

July 4

Dear Bailey,

First, HAPPY BIRTHDAY!!!! This is our only day off, so I'm answering your letter before classes begin again in the morning. That's how great a friend you are! Careful with Pete. Don't practice too much kissing because it might lead to something else. Sorry if I sound like your mother, but I only want you to BE CAREFUL.

I think I'm trying too hard. My timing's off and the dance master embarrassed me in front of the whole class yesterday. I just couldn't keep up and she really snapped at me. Some of the girls giggled (competition, you know). I could have sunk through the floor. I've got bruises all up and down my legs too, probably from too much barre work. I've been putting on stage makeup to cover the purple blotches, but my bunkmate noticed them last night and said I should tell our trainer. Fat chance! I'm not about to whine and complain about a few bruises.

Have you been to my house to visit Zorita? You said you would, so don't get too focused on Pete that you forget my poor lonely cat (who I'm sure misses me and wonders why I don't sleep in my bedroom every night).

Well, we're heading into town to listen to Pops in the Park and watch the fireworks show over the Potomac River. I plan to sleep in the van all the way there and back! Write soon!

Melinda (who wishes she felt better!)

TO: Lenny
SUBJECT: 911

Honey, I know you're 40,000 feet over the Atlantic right now, but you'll pick this up when you land. I've received a call from Washington. Melinda has collapsed and has been taken to Georgetown University Hospital. The doctors think it's exhaustion. I'm on my way to the airport and I'm frantic. I can't get to Washington fast enough. Call the hospital as soon as you get this. I don't care about the six-hour time difference. Dear God, I hope she's all right. I hate that she's alone until I get there.

Elana

Roses

❧

MELINDA'S DIARY

July 8

This has to be the MOST embarrassing thing that's ever happened to me! One minute I was in class doing a plié, my arms arched, my back perfectly aligned: the next minute, I woke up on the floor of the dance studio. Thinking back, I did feel dizzy and light-headed, and suddenly everything went to spinning. I felt hot all over and the music sounded like it was coming through a tunnel, then my stomach felt funny, and then came the floor and people screeching and the master holding my hands and rubbing my face. Someone stuck a wadded towel under my head and someone else lifted my feet. And voices kept saying, "Call an ambulance."

By the time the medics arrived, I was sitting up and feeling better, but I had to go to the ER and get checked out. The hospital called Mom, who came all the way up from Atlanta, and now I'm in a hospital room and she's huddling with some doctors in the hall. She said Dad's on his way back from Paris. I'm mortified! But I'm tired too. I'll bet I'm anemic, like Patti Johnson was last year. The doctors kept asking me questions in the ER and now it occurs to me that they were trying to find out if I'm a bulimic

UGH! How gross . . . sticking a finger down your throat to make yourself throw up just to lose weight. But I am losing weight. (I sort of fudged to the doctor when he asked my normal weight.) But I'm NOT bulimic. No way!

And the worst part of all is that everybody's conspiring against me to make me go home! I don't want to go home! Don't they understand? If I leave the school now, I'll never get asked back! This isn't fair. I've wanted this all my life and now it's going to be snatched away all because of a little fainting spell I had during class. I CAN'T STAND IT!!!!!!

TO: All Concerned
Subject: Melinda

I've created a special address heading—All Concerned—to keep everyone in our circle of family and friends updated about Melinda, and either I or Elana will give you information. PLEASE DON'T CALL THE HOSPITAL. We flew home with Melinda yesterday and checked her into Emory University Hospital, where she'll undergo tests for the next few days. She's running a fever, but she doesn't seem to have an illness—baffling. At the least, she's very anemic.

Elana is blaming herself for not catching Melinda's weight loss, bruising and excessive tiredness before Melinda took off to Washington. But our girl's never had a sick day in her life beyond those due to the common cold, so why should we have been suspicious?

We have great confidence in her doctors, especially her hematologist, Dr. Jan Powell, who we've been assured is one of the best in her field.

Melinda, Elana and I appreciate your prayers and thoughts, and as soon as we know what's going on, we'll let you know. In the meantime, keep praying.

Lenny

"Hi . . . is this really you, Melinda?"

"Bailey? Where are you?"

"The lobby. They won't let me upstairs to see you."

"Mom's turned into a real watchdog. She told the nurses' desk not to let anyone in. She's down in the cafeteria having dinner or she'd never have let me take this call."

"That's so mean!"

"She's not being mean, Bailey. She's just being Mom. It's good to hear your voice. . . ."

"Now don't start crying, or I will too. Can you tell me what's going on? I haven't got long to talk."

"How did you get here anyway?"

"Pete drove me. Now, tell me, what's happening?"

"I—I feel like a pincushion. They've drawn blood about a hundred times and sent me down for a CT scan—"

"A what?"

"It's a test—a full-body X ray."

"Oh. Did it hurt?"

"No . . . but *all* the needle sticks are awful!"

"When can you come home?"

"I don't know."

"Your mom asked me to take temporary custody of Zorita. She's being a good cat but she misses you."

"I miss her too. I miss everybody. Will you do me a favor?"

"Anything."

"E-mail Jesse. He's probably not on Dad's e-mail list. Jesse still thinks I'm in Washington."

"I'll e-mail him today. Now, don't cry or your

mom will pump you and you'll have to confess that I came here and talked to you. And my parents will *kill* me if they think I got into a car with Pete without their permission."

"Thanks for taking the chance, Bailey."

"Don't you know? 'Chance' is my middle name. I really want to see you."

"I'll beg Mom to bring you next time she comes. Maybe we'll know something by then. And . . . and thanks for telling Jesse for me."

TO: All Concerned
Subject: Tests

I'm letting those of you we love know all that is happening. They took Melinda down for a bone marrow aspiration today. I stood by her bed holding her hand while they told her about the procedure. It's horrible! They stick a long needle into her lower back between her vertebrae while she's curled into a fetal position. She'll only have a local anesthetic to numb the skin and she has to lie stone-still. One of the nurses said that Melinda could hold her hands and squeeze as hard as she wanted. She said that Melinda could yell or cry—anything except move. I begged them to let me go along, but Melinda wouldn't have any of it. She looked at me and said, "Mom, I'm not a baby." I watched them roll her away while I cried. Doesn't she know? She's MY baby. Please keep praying. We don't know what else to do but wait and hope.

Elana

TO: Jesse Rose
Subject: Melinda

Hi—

This is Bailey, Melinda's friend. Remember me? Well, it doesn't matter. What does is this: I'm writing you because Melinda asked me to. She's in the hospital. Now, don't freak. We still don't know too much about what's wrong with her. It's got something to do with her blood, because that's what they keep testing. Here's what happened. She fainted in ballet class in D.C. and got rushed to a hospital. Her mother went to Washington and flew back with her to Atlanta, where Melinda got checked into another hospital.

There she lies until the doctors figure out what's wrong. I've talked to her and she sounded scared. Just as soon as I know something, I'll e-mail you—you can contact me anytime. The important thing is that we help Melinda get through this really bad time, because we're her two best friends in the whole world. That's what she told me once.

Bailey

MELINDA'S DIARY

July 11

They stuck a needle in my back today. I couldn't see it, but I really felt it . . . like it was sucking out my insides. It hurt so bad. I tried not to cry. I squeezed the nurse's hands so hard that she yelped and I felt bad even though she said it was okay. I wished I'd let Mom come with me for the test, but I didn't want her any more upset. She looks like she's going to cry all the time. Dad looks like he hasn't slept in days. I hope whatever's wrong with me isn't bad. Please, God, don't let it be bad.

TO: Ann
Subject: Apology

I am so sorry you were inadvertently left off our e-mail news list. Please forgive us. Lenny and I have been distraught over Melinda and we're not thinking clearly. The second I heard Jesse's voice on our answering machine, I realized what had happened. Poor kid! He sounded upset. I had forgotten how long he and Melinda have been friends. Of course the news hit him hard. Melinda said she'd asked Bailey to get the word to him.

Well, you're in the e-mail loop now and just as soon as we know something, we'll send out the word. I hate the worried look on her doctor's face. I know that whatever is wrong, it's serious—much more than a case of severe anemia like they'd first suspected.

Tell Jesse that Melinda will be in touch, because they have computers here at the hospital and patients can use the Internet and e-mail. We just found this out today.

Elana

**UNIVERSITY PATHOLOGY
CONSULTANTS**

121 East 18th Street, Suite 318
Atlanta, GA 30020
Phone: (800) 555-4567 Fax: (800) 555-4568

BONE MARROW PATHOLOGY REPORT

Referring Physician: Janet Powell, M.D.
Specimen Number: JL01-99437
Hematology Associates
Emory University Hospital, Suite 2010
Atlanta, GA 30020

Date Collected: 7/11
Date Received: 7/11
Date Reported: 7/12

Diagnosis: Acute Lymphoblastic Leukemia

Gross Description
The specimen consists of 5 slides and 2 additional aliquots of 3 cc each, labeled "Bone Marrow Aspirate, Melinda Skye."

Microscopic Description:
The bone marrow aspirate demonstrates extensive hypercellularity with normal bone marrow elements essentially replaced by infiltrating lymphoblasts. There are multiple mitotic figures seen. The lymphoblasts demonstrate a high nuclear/cytoplasm ratio and clumped nuclear chromatin. Some nuclei display a folded appearance. Scattered among the abnormal cells are small numbers of erythroid, myeloid, and megakaryocytic cells.

Flow cytometric immunophenotypic studies demonstrated a

population of beta lymphocytes, which expressed the CD19 and CD20 antigens, and were weakly positive for CD10 (CALLA) antigens.

Cytochemistry was positive for TdT, further corroborating a lymphoblastic process and poor prognosis.

The findings are consistent with acute lymphoblastic leukemia.

Stephen R. Jones, M.D.
Pathologist

TO: Jesse
Subject: The Final Word

Hi. . . . I'm writing this from a hospital computer. My fingers are shaking and I'm crying. Dr. Powell gave us the results of my tests today. She told us what's wrong with me. I have leukemia, Jesse. I have cancer.

Melinda

TO: My Ballerina Girl, Melinda
Subject: Sad

Ever since Bailey sent me the e-mail telling me you were in the hospital, my worried imagination has been going crazy. I thought about all the things that could have made you sick—really bad flu, or some weird disease. I never thought it could be cancer. You're too young to get cancer! I know cancer isn't contagious: it can't be "caught" like a cold. But why you, Melinda? It shouldn't happen to someone as wonderful as you!

Mom says you have a good doctor and that you'll get the best care in the world. PLEASE write me often—every day if you feel like it—and let me know how you're doing. I think of you every minute of every day.

Jesse

P.S. I'm sending you something to cheer you up as soon as I get the money together!

TO: Jesse
Subject: Just to Talk

I don't know why I got cancer, and don't think I haven't asked! The doctors don't know, Mom and Dad don't know. Maybe it's just bad luck. But whatever it is, I sure do hate it. This doesn't seem real. I keep thinking this is a bad dream and I'll wake up any minute. But I don't wake up. And I have to take chemo treatments, which scare me to death. Gee, did I really mean to write "death"? Oh, Jesse, I wish I could see you. . . . I wish this wasn't happening to me. . . . I just want to go home and have everything the way it used to be.

Melinda

TO: All Concerned
Subject: Doctor's Report

Now that we know the worst, we're hoping for the best.

First of all, thank you for all the cards, notes and gifts you've sent Melinda since we learned the news. Her hospital room looks like an annex for a boutique! Really, your generosity is much appreciated and has cheered Melinda greatly.

Melinda has been transferred to All-Children's Hospital, where she'll be supervised by a team of physicians in a state-of-the-art complex associated with St. Jude, the famous children's cancer research hospital in Memphis. She has a hematologist, an oncologist, a psychiatrist (for adjustment to the diagnosis), a nutritionist, a social worker—in short, a whole team of people to help her cope with her cancer (the latest concept in treating the patient as a whole, not piecemeal). A good idea, I guess, but there are a lot of new people in our lives, the kind that parents hope they never have to meet under circumstances we never think we'll face.

Melinda had a blood transfusion to elevate her red cell count and she looks and feels much better. She's also on antibiotics to deal with the bone marrow infection and is fever-free for the first time in days. Tomorrow she'll begin her first round of chemo, which her oncologist, Dr. Neely, hopes will put her into remission. Once they adjust her levels of chemo, which is pretty potent stuff, she'll get to return home. Then she'll go onto outpatient status. She'll have to come in for more treatments (the doctors call them proto-cols), be hooked up to an infusion pump for a few hours at a time and have more chemo dumped into her via IV, but at least we'll be able to take her home after each treatment.

The goal is to get her into remission and keep her there. Some patients never have a relapse. Others can have one after being cancer-free for a few years. A patient is considered "cured" if there are no relapses after five years. Frankly, there's so much to learn and adjust to that we're all overwhelmed. I asked Dr. Neely how we'll get through this and he said, "The same way every-one else gets through it—one day at a time."

More later,
Lenny

═══════════════════════════════

MELINDA'S DIARY

July 15

The chemo started today. IVs in my arm, wads of pills in my mouth, a whole schedule of stuff that is poisonous. Dr. Neely says it has to be strong enough to kill the cancer cells. I hope it doesn't kill me along with it.

I asked him if I was going to lose my hair. He said, "Maybe not." I sure hope he's right. I imagine a bald ballerina and I start to cry. The doctors told me that I can return to dancing as soon as I'm in remission and feel up to it. They want me to be physically active. But no one understands how hard dance is and how far behind I'll have fallen. Where will I ever get the energy to compete again? I'm sick to my stomach and have to stop writing. WHY IS THIS HAPPENING TO ME????

TO: Jesse
Subject: Melinda, of course

I wish I could answer the questions you ask me, but I can't. Yes, she's really sick. Yes, she's really unhappy. I don't know about the dying part, but I won't even THINK that! I did get to go up and visit her and she looks pretty good. Skinnier and paler, but still like Melinda. Just to prove it, I'll bring a camera next time I go and take some pics of her and her hospital room and I'll send them to you. I'll be your eyes and ears, Jesse. I promise!

Bailey

Elana's Journal

Midnight

I bought this journal today because I have to start writing things down...private things that I can't share in coast-to-coast e-mails, not with Lenny, certainly not with Melinda. I see my daughter, my dear child, writing in her little diary that she puts away and locks if anyone comes into the room while she's writing in it (as if I'd ever read her personal and private diary!). I know it's a release for her. The psychiatrist, Dr. Sanchez, was pleased when she learned that Melinda has the habit of keeping a diary. She told me that "journaling" is therapeutic. God knows I need such therapy myself, so I'll give it a try.

I can't believe this is happening to our child. Cancer. The word alone sends shivers of pure terror through me. But Melinda is such a brave little soldier. She goes through every treatment without complaint. I believe it's due to years of discipline from ballet. Ah . . . her ballet. She gets upset with me if I even mention it. Competing and losing a part to another is one thing; having your dream snatched away so cruelly is quite another. She doesn't deserve this.

I must stop thinking negatively. Melinda WILL dance again. She WILL beat leukemia. She absolutely, positively WILL. I can't afford to think otherwise. Lenny has his job to keep his mind occupied. But my job, my joy, has always been Melinda. How ironic that in my "volunteer" mode, I chaired events that raised thousands for this hospital. Now our Melinda is a recipient of all that effort and money. And me? I feel "out of work." How can I let Melinda know that I want her to need me as much as I need her?

MELINDA'S DIARY

July ??? (Lost track of time, but it seems like forever.)

I felt pretty good today. No nausea, and the food even tasted all right. (Some of the meds I take give food a funny—like peculiar, not ha-ha—taste). I can't believe all the presents and flowers and cards I've gotten! My friends from school, dance class, relatives . . . Mom had to take stuff home. Dad sent me a HUGE bouquet. Bailey gave me a white teddy bear with a red heart sewn into its fur. But my best present is a whole dozen pink roses from Jesse. They are so beautiful. His card said, "Roses go to the prettiest flower of all. From a Rose (admirer)." Isn't that sweet? I'd like to see him face to face . . . (before my hair falls out—if it does).

Bailey says she and Jesse e-mail each other regularly to "discuss" me. I'm not sure I like that too much. But it sounds petty to say anything about it, because both are my friends and I know they just want to help. Bailey brought me pictures of Zorita and I got a big lump in my throat because I want to go home and be normal again.

Will I ever be normal again?

Felt rotten today. Threw up all my supper. Refused ice cream for bedtime snack. Sleep is all I want.

Mom practically lives here at the hospital with me. Sometimes I wish she'd just go away. Other times, I want to crawl in her lap like a baby with a boo-boo. I haven't written Jesse in days, because I just don't feel like it. He probably hates me.

A new horror started today—sores inside my mouth from the chemo. They hurt so bad, I can't eat anything. I HATE my life!

Some therapist visited today. She taught me about imaging. I'm supposed to imagine my white blood cells "eating" the cancer cells. Tonight I played a video game with some super-graphic, kick-butt woman wiping out a nest of robotic aliens. I pretended she was ripping through my bloodstream destroying cancer cells. I got the second-highest score according to the chart of those who've played the game in the past month. Hail, Melinda!

Woke up this morning and found a huge clump of my hair on the pillow. I cried. I guess I won't be one of the "lucky ones" who keep their hair. Mom said that because my hair is so thick it's hardly noticeable, but I notice it! I told her I want it all cut off.

Mom brought her hairdresser, David, to the hospital today and he sat me in a chair and cut my hair into a super-short pixie cut. I look so different. But at least now if it all falls out, I'll be used to seeing it short. Plus, now there won't be as much to fall when it leaves my head.

Bailey came up and went on and on about how "cute" I looked. She said the new cut makes my eyes look huge. I told her thanks. I think it makes me look like a refugee from a concentration camp. Maybe that's because I've lost twelve pounds in two weeks. But I just can't eat anything!

July 30

Dear Melinda,
  I've given up sending you e-mails because you never answer them. The only news I get is from Bailey. Even your dad's stopped sending e-mail updates. I can't stand being cut off. Please don't abandon me.

Jesse

MELINDA'S DIARY

July 31

I'm ashamed of myself. I've been thinking about myself and what was happening to me so much that I forgot to really look around and see everybody else stuck in this hospital. Mom rolled me out into the halls in a wheelchair (THAT sure felt weird, rolling instead of walking), and I saw so many others with cancer like me—some a whole lot younger and a whole lot worse off!

The little kids are the saddest to see. Most of them are bald and they look so thin—I call it "the chemo look." One boy who's maybe four or five was sitting in the children's rec room coloring. There he was, an IV hooked to his arm, another to his chest, his little bald head bent over a coloring book. The crayons were spread all over the table, his tiny hand was holding a brown crayon, and he was coloring as if it was the most normal thing in the world. I just sat there and watched him and felt tears sliding down my face. It made me so sad. He's like any other little kid, except he isn't. He has cancer. Like me.

I went back to my room and cried for an hour.

TO: Jesse
Subject: Apology

I got your card and note and I'm sorry I've not been a very good friend. So much has been happening to me that I lost sight of some of the things in my life that really count. You're at the top of that list. I had Mom bring your framed picture from my dresser to the hospital and now I can see you every day and remind myself that what's happening to me is also happening, in a way, to my family and friends.

Dad uses words like "brave" and "courageous" when he e-mails people about me, but that's not really true. I'm neither of those things. I'm scared and angry and very unhappy. I don't know why anyone wants to be around me, because I'm so mean to people—especially the people who matter the most to me, like you and Mom and Dad. Even Bailey has been "busy" lately. Oh, she calls and has come to visit a couple of times, but the truth is we don't have much to talk about these days. My world is so small now. Hers is normal.

Dancing, the thing I once did that made my life

mine, lies in ruins, like a crumbled wreck. I'd better stop writing because I'm getting melodramatic. I won't stop writing you ever again. That's a promise.

Melinda

TO: Jesse
Subject: Friendship

OK . . . to answer your latest e-mail accusation: I AM NOT ABANDONING MELINDA. (I'm shouting this answer to you.) For starters, I have to baby-sit my twin sisters (HALF sisters!) this summer while Mom and Bill work, so I don't have much time to go to the hospital and back. The hospital is miles from here and when traffic's bad (which is almost all the time in Atlanta), it takes almost an hour just to get there. That leaves me only weekends to visit her. Most of the time, Mom and Bill have other things to do on weekends, so they can't take me and it's a rare day they let me get into a car with teen drivers (like Pete, my boyfriend, whom they don't like me dating, but that's another story!).

So you see, crabbing me out for not visiting

Melinda more often isn't very fair. Yes, I know, now that I've explained everything, you're sorry.

Apology accepted.

Friends(?),
Bailey

MELINDA'S DIARY

August 1

Mrs. Houston brought Tanya and Kathi for a visit today. They looked SO good! So healthy. I wanted to crawl under the covers and hide because I do not look good or healthy. They kept talking about how much everyone missed me and how poorly they do in class without me there to "push them to perfection." I know they're just giving me a line to make me feel better, but it was good to hear anyway.

Mrs. Houston says that just as soon as I'm able to resume classes, she'll work extra with me so that I can get back into shape more quickly. She said that she's saving a part in this year's Nutcracker and that dancers from the Denver Dance Company will be a part of our production. And that includes Natalie Blackbird, one of the best ballerinas in the country! I promised all of them that I'll be back real soon. I mean it too! I will!

Elana's Journal

August 1

It's 2:30 a.m. and I'm sitting in the hospital chapel because I can't sleep. I've stayed in the room with Melinda most nights (there's a large chair that makes up into a bed, a lumpy bed), but once she falls asleep, I lie there wide awake. I come here because it's open around the clock and I find it quiet and peaceful. The room feels like a refuge to me. Behind the altar area is a beautiful stained-glass window of healing hands touching through a rainbow. The window's lit artificially from behind so that it looks as if it's never dark outside. It helps offset the darkness inside my heart.

Melinda's been here two weeks already and still no remission. I thought it would happen more quickly. She's getting the newest drugs, the most powerful weapons science has against leukemia, but remission remains elusive. Her cancer still lurks, like a crouching lion, in her blood tests. How do I fight an enemy I can't see? How do I balance being Melinda's mother and her guardian? I know I hold on too tight. I can't help it.

I come here to pray. For strength. For healing. For wisdom. Sometimes the night seems endless and the days too rushed. Oh, what I'd give to go back to my mundane life of schlepping my daughter to dance rehearsals, of grocery shopping, summer cook-outs, and busywork. I miss Lenny when he flies out for days at a time. I miss my life. I want Melinda well and whole. And home.

Yes, I want her home!

MELINDA'S DIARY

August 4

I promise to be nicer to Mom. It's not her fault I'm stuck here (unless leukemia turns out to be genetic, then it IS all her fault! A little humor). I don't know why I take it out on her. I can see how it hurts her, but I'm nasty anyway. Bad ME! But I will do better. I swear!

AUDIO TRANSCRIPTION BY
DR. LEIGH NEELY, ONCOLOGIST,
FOR INSERTION INTO MEDICAL
FILE OF MELINDA SKYE:

Melinda Skye's case continues to prove stubborn. I'm adjusting her protocols and will introduce SGX-243. It's experimental, but she fits the parameters of suggested use and I believe her case calls for it. Will monitor her closely for the adverse side effects mentioned in the drug studies. Her family continues to be supportive and open to treatment options. Melinda is a strong-willed girl with above-average intelligence that will serve her well during the difficult months ahead. Submitted: 8:10 P.M., August 4

MELINDA'S DIARY

August (whatever!)

I absolutely, positively, categorically WILL NOT spend my birthday in this hospital. I told Dr. Neely this morning to either fix me or cut me loose, because I want OUT. He said he's trying something new. I hope so, because I'm so sick of this place I could scream.

Elana's Journal

August 5

Dr. Neely told us that he wants to try a new drug on Melinda because he's not getting the "required results" from other drugs. The new medication is part of a clinical trial and, according to him, results have been promising. It's a hard choice to make. Lenny's more daring than I and he wants to give the go-ahead. I'm more hesitant.

The side effects sound grim—weight gain, bleeding gums, sudden nosebleeds, brittle bones. The

brittle bones part scares me the most. Doesn't anyone realize that she can't ever dance if her bones
begin to break? Lenny reminds me that these are
potential side effects, and that Melinda may not
experience any of them. Dr. Neely says she'll be
closely monitored and that once remission is
achieved, the dosage will be decreased and eventu-
ally he will wean her off of it and onto a more
standardized regimen.

My foot-dragging has caused friction between
Lenny and me. I don't like that, because we really
need to lean on each other. I don't know what to
do. Lenny wants it. Dr. Neely wants it. Melinda
wants it. I'm the only holdout. I want Melinda
well, but at what cost?

MELINDA'S DIARY

August 10

That Bailey is such a nut! Today she brought a
stack of teen magazines and her entire brand-new
school wardrobe to model for me. She had drawn
up a chart listing the clothes and three columns:

Consider It, Burn It, Buy It. As she modeled each piece, I checked off my opinion. Then she said she'd go shopping for me and get the things I liked best. That way, I'll have new clothes for school without ever setting foot inside a store. And of course, they'll be "of the moment" because Bailey's so hip about fashion.

It really perked my day. Even Mom got into it and offered her opinions. She said she'd give Bailey the money to get whatever I wanted. What we didn't say out loud is that I won't be starting school on time. I'm trying not to think about that because we have to "wait and see" until I know how I handle my treatments. (Or is it how they handle me?)

I started the new drug combos today and I think I feel better already. (That's the power of positive thinking!) Mom finally caved, but I know she's not thrilled about it. Dad and I ganged up on her—unfair, but necessary. It's MY body and MY disease. I said, "Experiment on me. Please. Just get me out of here!"

It looks like I won't be shaving my legs for a long, long time. "Chemo hair loss" means more than saying goodbye to the hair on top of my head. My eyebrows are gone and so are my eyelashes (not to *mention body hair in very private places!). Dr. Neely says it'll grow back when chemo's over, but for now I look smooth and round as a pumpkin. I'm glad I'm in the school's homebound program and everyone can't see what a freak-a-zoid I've become. I refuse to go to school until I look better NO MAT-TER WHAT.*

TO: Ballerina Girl
Subject: New Meds

I'm betting this new drug will be the one! I just feel it deep inside me. I've got my fingers crossed for you.

Got a long letter from my dad saying how much he wants me to be a part of his family. He says that Donna's boys are like sons to him, but I'm his REAL son and that makes him proud. I want to say, "Well, how about my REAL mother? She's half of me too." He can't just take the part he wants and forget the part he doesn't want. Life doesn't work that way. I haven't written him back because I honestly don't know what to say. He expects to walk back into my life after all this time and pick up where we left off. It can't be

done. I'm not seven anymore. And he's a different person than the one I worshiped back
then.

Write soon,
Jesse

TO: Jesse
Subject: Parents

I know what you're saying. There was a time
when I thought Mom and Dad knew everything,
but now I know they don't. Sometimes they look
as scared as I feel. That rocked me the first time
I realized it. Mom still sleeps here at night. Can
you believe it? I've told her it's okay for her to go
home and come back the next day. She won't.
Then it hit me: She can't make my leukemia go
away and this is all she has to offer me. Her
presence. So I've stopped telling her I'm fine
without her at night. She needs to be here for
reasons of her own.

Maybe your dad needs to feel like he's still a part
of your life instead of the parent who checked
out and missed all those years of you growing

up. Maybe he's trying to make up for what he can't go back and change.

Forgive me. I've been talking to Dr. Sanchez (the shrink) too much! I see deep meaning in everything. Too much time to lie around thinking . . . that's all.

Philosophically yours,
Melinda

AUDIO TRANSCRIPTION BY
DR. NEELY FOR INSERTION INTO
MEDICAL FILE OF MELINDA SKYE:

Latest labs indicate that SGX-243 is working for Melinda Skye. There's a dramatic turn-around. Her spinal fluid is clear, her white blood count is near normal, and healthy red cells are proliferating. While I'm heartened by the results, I know the treatment can't be repeated. Let's hope it holds. Submitted: 10:07 P.M. August 20

TO: All Concerned
Subject: Success!

Finally. The new drug is turning the tide and we've achieved remission, so it looks as if she'll be able to come home before her birthday. This is a banner day. Elana and I can't wait to get our little girl out of this place, and Melinda can't wait to leave.

We've got a schedule set up for continued chemo over the next six months, but maybe the worst is over and future tests will show that Melinda's cancer-free. I believe she's weathered the storm and permanent remission will be achieved. She's suffered enough and now it's time to pick up our lives, which have been on hold ever since this nightmare began.

Thanks again for your prayers. Keep it up!
Lenny & Elana

MELINDA'S DIARY

August 25

I can't believe I'm sitting in my own bedroom writing this. Everything looks just the way I left it before I took off to Washington, but it's kind of unreal too. I'm so used to the hospital, the nurses' comings and goings, the other kids, the smells of the halls, the rattle of the food carts, the doctors dropping by twice a day. The gang on my floor threw me a little party before we left—very sweet. There were balloons and cupcakes and there was a clown to entertain the little kids. I was the only teen up there and the younger kids looked up to me. Keisha, who's six, even cried, but I promised to visit when I return for my treatments. (Maybe she'll be out by then, I hope, I hope.)

Zorita was sitting on my bed when I got here. Bailey had tied a bow with a bell around her collar and she looked really cute. I think she's forgiven me for leaving her for so long, because she curled up on my pillow like she used to do.

When I think over the last two months, they seem like a bad dream. But they weren't. I know they really happened, because there's a shunt in my chest for the upcoming chemo treatments. It's ugly, but I can hide it under my clothes. I'm tired now and I'm going to bed with my cat.

Elana's Journal

August 25

This will be quick. Part of me is elated to have my baby back in her room down the hall. The other part is scared witless. At the hospital, nurses were close at hand, so if Melinda had any problems I could run and get them. Here, it's only me and Lenny. Maybe only me because Lenny travels so much.

Lenny programmed all the important phone numbers into our telephones and I have lists of emergency measures to take if something I can't handle happens, but still it's frightening to be the sole one in charge. I think Melinda senses my fear and ineptitude.

I pray that everything goes well. Melinda's been through so much ... TOO much for a girl who'll be fourteen in a few days. She's changed since June, and seems older, more stoic. I miss my little girl.

TO: Ann
Subject: Melinda's Birthday

When I asked Melinda what she wanted for her birthday, she said, "I'd like to be cancer-free, go to Paris with a dance troupe, have boobs bigger than apricots, and see Jesse Rose." At this time, the first three things on her list are out of reach. But seeing Jesse isn't. If you're willing to let him come, we'd love to fly him to Atlanta for a visit. As Lenny says, "A lot of things in Melinda's life are out of my control, but a nonstop flight across the country for one of her friends isn't one of them!"

I know school might have started (it has here and Melinda cried because she couldn't go), but if you'll let Jesse come for even a few days, Lenny and I will be ever so grateful. Please think about it and call us. If the answer's yes, we'll arrange everything.

Elana (with fingers crossed)

TO: Elana and Lenny
Subject: Melinda's Birthday

How could I say no to such a heartfelt request? Besides, if I did, my son would never speak to me again! Plus, he might stow away on a plane and go anyway!

Yes, school has started, but so what? Jesse's had a terrible summer. He talked about Melinda constantly and so wanted to see her. He had little to do after returning from New York and I felt really sorry for him moping around while I worked. Don't tell Melinda, but he sold his skateboard and some of his baseball card collection to kids here at the apartment complex in order to send her flowers and the few presents that he's bought for her birthday.

I wish I could make arrangements for the flight myself but I could not financially afford for him to do this. He can stay up to a week, but don't let him wear out his welcome. And thank you. This visit will mean all the world to him.

Ann

————— ❧ —————

MELINDA'S DIARY

August 30, 11 P.M.

Seeing Jesse again after all this time has been strange and wonderful at once. I've been a nervous wreck ever since Mom and Dad announced that he was coming. I was glad, but not thrilled, and I only wished they had asked me first instead of surprising me with the news. Not that I didn't want to see him—I did. But let's face it: I'm not at my best. Chemo has left its ugly mark. After weeks of being sick and burpy, I'm now swinging the other way: F-A-T. Dr. Neely told me this might happen (I still take a handful of pills every day plus the sucky chemo treatments), but I really didn't think I'd look so freaky.

My face looks like a Moon Pie—round and flat, really gross. Bailey says I'm overreacting, but she's not the one swollen up like a toad. Then I learned that Jesse was coming. I wanted to put a bag over my head. What was Mom thinking?

I was so nervous going to the airport tonight to meet Jesse's plane that I was sick to my stomach. Dad parked the car and we walked into the terminal. The monitors flashed that Jesse's flight from LA had landed, so we waited near the security entrance. My mouth was so dry I couldn't even swallow. I saw him coming, because he was holding a really big teddy bear. He looks like his pictures, but taller, and his eyes are still so very, very blue. When Jesse saw me, his face turned beet red. (He was probably wishing he could get right back on the plane and head home!) We just sort of stood there staring at each other like a couple of stupid cows, then Mom started gabbing blah-blah-blah—all the way through the baggage claim, the walk to the parking lot and the whole ride back to the house! There we sat in the back of her SUV, me hugging one car door, and Jesse the other while Dad drove and Mom talked. I thought I was going to scream, "Please be quiet!" but I bit my tongue. She was ruining everything! Just talking and talking, and me and Jesse embarrassed because we really didn't know what to say to each other—not that we had much of a chance with Mom's mouth running. Jesse and I had "talked" through cards and e-mails, but suddenly, in person, we were strangers.

Just as I was considering opening the door and hurling myself into traffic, I felt Jesse reach across *the seat in the dark and his fingers touch mine. I felt frozen in place, but his fingers warmed mine and soon I started to relax. We sat that way for the rest of the ride to the house, Jesse's hand holding mine and Mom blabbering about everything and nothing. But by then, I didn't care. Jesse was here. And I was with him.*

<Bailey> I know it's late, but I'm looking out my window and I see that your bedroom light's on. Is your computer on? Can you e-mail me right back? Is Jesse there?

<Melinda> Yes, I'm here and totally awake. I heard my computer e-mail bell ding and was glad it was you. . . . Yes, Jesse's here in his old room in the basement. He said it was like coming home.

<Bailey> Tell me EVERYTHING! What's he like? Do you still like-like him? Details, I want details.

\<Melinda\> He's cute and a little shy. Not that I blame him. Mom practically talked our ears off from the airport to the house. Then when we got here, she sat us in the kitchen for cookies and milk! Can you believe it? Just like we were in grade school. I wanted to crawl under the table, I was so embarrassed. Finally, Dad said it was time to "turn in" . . . another embarrassing moment. He marched Jesse down to the guest room. Doesn't he know that Jesse's like three hours behind us and probably isn't one bit sleepy? Good thing there's a TV down there.

\<Bailey\> What are you and Jesse going to do tomorrow on your birthday?

\<Melinda\> Mom and Dad are taking us to Six Flags (where I plan to lose them in the crowds).

<Bailey> Can I bring your
present over in the morning?
And meet Jesse?

<Melinda> Come around 9:30,
or you'll miss us.

<Bailey> See you tomorrow!
And happy birthday in advance.
Night, now. (And NO sleepwalking
down to Jesse's room.)

Elana's Journal

August 30

11:30 p.m.

*I got under Melinda's skin tonight with my in-
cessant talking from the second Jesse arrived. She
kept giving me furtive looks and I knew I was
overdoing it, but I couldn't seem to control my
mouth. Even Lenny mentioned it to me when we
were alone, saying he felt "sorry for the boy" because of my verbal bombardment. Maybe it's the*

strain of the past weeks, but I vow I won't do it again.

Seeing Melinda and Jesse together again brought back memories of the two of them in grade school. They were both so cute and practically inseparable. I loved having him around and so did Melinda. So many memories...

She's grown up so fast. My daughter, my child... so pretty and smart. And burdened with cancer. It's not fair!

HAPPY BIRTHDAY!
To the world's best daughter . . . with all our love, Mom and Dad
P.S. There's a little surprise for you in the garage.

MELINDA'S DIARY

August 31 (My Birthday!!!!!)

This has been the best day of my life (so far)! At breakfast, I got Mom and Dad's card and let them blindfold me and lead me out to the garage. When Mom removed the blindfold, I almost fainted.

They'd had the garage converted into a dance/ exercise room for me! Air-conditioning, heating, a partial wooden floor, a mirrored wall and a barre so that I can work out on my own. Also, a treadmill and StairMaster to build up my endurance. This is wonderful! Now I can go at my own pace and return to the studio when I'm in better shape. I just screeched and hugged them both. I asked Dad, "But what about the cars?" (He's been known to obsess about his little BMW.) He said, "A little exposure to the elements never hurt a car." And Mother said, "He's been thinking of trading it in anyway for something more suitable for a man in his forties." And they gave each other a little look that said they were pleased to have surprised me so totally.

Jesse tried the treadmill and the StairMaster, but he said he'd leave the barre work to me. Then Bailey came over and we had to go through the squealing and excitement again. She met Jesse and pronounced him "really cute" to me when he wasn't around to overhear. I don't know why I care what Bailey thinks of him, but I do. She gave me a really cool top and a beaded bracelet for gifts.

We went to Six Flags, but I was really wiped out, so I wasn't much fun. Mom wanted to take me home, but I absolutely refused, so Dad and Jesse went on the rides together. Mom got some good pics of them and they both looked like they were having a good time. When we came home, I threw up (sure don't want Jesse to know that part), then I crashed and slept until about seven o'clock. I crawled downstairs and they were waiting to eat. I voted for pizza, and after it came I ate a piece and felt better. Mom brought out a cake (angel food with white coconut icing, my favorite) and lit candles, and Mom, Dad and Jesse sang to me. I still can't believe he's really here!

Jesse and I finally got to be alone at about ten o'clock. We sat out on the porch in the swing watching fireflies.

Jesse asked, "Do you know why fireflies light up?"

"No," I said.

"It's the way they tell each other that they're available," he said.

"Nice trick," I said.

"See?" he said, pointing into the darkness where the bugs kept glowing on and off. "That one's saying, 'Find me, find me.' And another is saying, 'Here I am, here I am.' "

Jesse took my hand and my heart started to pound like a drum. He reached under the swing and brought out a box. (I must have been asleep when he put it there.) He said, "Happy birthday."

I unwrapped it and held up a beautiful ballerina figurine. She's perfect and very fragile.

"It's made of porcelain," he said. "That's supposed to be nice stuff."

I told him how much I LOVED it. I wanted to hug him, but I was too shy. Good thing too, 'cause Mom came out and said it was time for a snack (our code for "time to take more pills").

The ballerina is on my dresser, in the place of honor she deserves, and I see her whenever I look up.

I've known Jesse forever . . . I wonder if what I felt for him tonight is l-o-v-e? Mom would say I'm too young to be in love, but I don't know. . . . He's very special to me. He makes me glow.

Elana's Journal

August 31, 11 P.M.

Tonight, as I looked at Melinda and Jesse together, I saw a woman inside my child. And I saw how Jesse looks at her, with adoration, pure sweet adoration.

He doesn't appear to see the effects of her cancer

on her, which is a miracle, I think. I'm grateful that he has been so kind to her. How awful it would been if he had acted like a jerk and rejected her. How would she have accepted his rejection? It would have crushed her. If he chooses not to stay in touch once he returns to California, I'll understand. But until that happens, I bless that boy.

If I could put the joy of this day in a bottle and save it, I would. It helps balance out those days in the hospital when all seemed bleak and lost. My child is growing up ... and as her mother, I'm torn between wanting it and dreading it. I wish my mother were still alive and that I could talk to her.

Happy birthday, Melinda, my daughter, my child. I love you so very much.

———————— ❧ ————————

TO: Mom
Subject: My Visit

I'm using Melinda's computer to write this while she's napping. Her mom said it's OK, that my tapping on computer keys won't wake her. I like being here and seeing her again. I was afraid during the flight that she'd think I was some nutty kid from a past life she'd HAD to invite just to be nice. I was afraid she didn't really want me here but had agreed to my visit so she wouldn't hurt her parents' feelings. She's told me though that she's glad I'm here, and that she hopes we can be friends forever. Nice, huh?

I like her mom and dad as much as I ever did (although her mom talks a lot, but DON'T tell her I said so). You should see the way they fixed up their garage so that Melinda can begin dancing again! BTW, her dad's taking us all to a Braves game Friday night (if Melinda feels like it). He's on flight duty now, but he'll be home tomorrow.

Hope you aren't missing me too much. I'll fly home next Saturday and will send the schedule once Mr. Skye sets it up. Wish I could stay longer.

Jesse

===

MELINDA'S DIARY

September 1

Tomorrow is Labor Day, and we're going out on the lake in the sailboat. Jesse's never sailed before even though he lives in California. He leaves Saturday and I'm really going to miss him, but I'm glad he won't be around to witness my further decline. I'm getting fatter by the day and the new meds make me really tired and cranky. I have a chemo session next Friday and will begin the homebound program next Monday. Not looking forward to either!

Bailey says school's boring (her usual take on school), but that she's been looking around for a new boyfriend because Pete's going to the community college and doesn't have time (or interest) for her these days. Poor Bailey—she wants a steady boyfriend so much. Hope she gets one soon.

I keep trying to stay dance-fit. Going up on pointe is killer! My feet are so out of shape. I have to build up the calluses again, and no matter how tight I wrap my little footies, they still hurt. My toenails began to bleed from the pressure of toe work. Jesse wanted to get Mom, but I grabbed him. "She'll make me stop," I said. "I have to keep going."

He said, "Maybe you should stop."

"I'll never get into shape if I don't toughen up," I said. "No pain, no gain."

We were standing real close and that's when he saw the shunt taped to my chest. I was mortified. I explained that it has a shut-off valve but is connected to a portal vein, and that it's there so the doctors won't have to find a vein every time I go for chemo. Veins often collapse because the chemo is so strong. I was afraid he would be grossed out, but he only asked questions and studied it. He made me feel that wearing a shunt is the most normal thing in the world.

He told me that science is his favorite subject, especially biology (he's in some kind of accelerated program in his school and he attends a few classes at the community college. This was news because he's never mentioned it before). I told him, "Way to go," and he grinned (which almost stopped my heart). I thought I knew everything about him, but now I know that I don't. Which is fine with me. It's sort of like digging through a box and finding something unexpected that makes you feel happy.

<Melinda> While you get to hang with Jesse, I am stuck in classes. Not that I'm jealous. Anyway, big news: Pete is definitely history and I've tumbled for Kerry Robinson. I should have mentioned sooner that he and I have been flirting in class (we have two together!) and hanging out in the halls, but I wanted to wait until it was a *fait accompli* (see, I AM learning something in French class).

<Bailey> Kerry is totally a jock and totally popular. I'm so happy!

<Melinda> Congrats on landing Kerry. What happened to Allison, his main squeeze from last year?

<Bailey> She got preggie! Kerry swears not by him.

<Melinda> And you believe him? They were joined at the hip all last year.

\<Bailey\> Sure I believe him. Why shouldn't I?

\<Melinda\> Don't get offended. Just be careful. Actually, I feel sorry for Allison. Don't you? She's only fourteen and "with child." What will she do? Do you know?

\<Bailey\> I don't know anything about Allison's story. Don't worry, I'll be careful. How about you? Are you and Jesse still "just good friends"? Any mouth-to-mouth action yet?

\<Melinda\> When something exciting happens, I'll tell you. I have to go now. Movie about to start on the VCR for Jesse and me. Popcorn, sodas, ice cream—no wonder I weigh a ton. But NO parents hanging over us. Mom and Dad went out for the evening.

Melinda's Diary

September 2 (Labor Day)

We had a good breeze on Lake Lanier, and the sailboat skimmed along like a waterbird. Jesse was impressed. I told him that sailing is the best way to ride the wind and he agreed. Dad showed him how to trim the sails, swing the boom, and tack to move the boat across the lake. Mom packed a picnic and we dropped anchor in the middle of the lake and feasted. I had to cover up most of the day and slather on the sunscreen because some of the meds I'm taking interact with the sun. I really didn't mind since I didn't want Jesse to see me in a swimsuit in my present blubbery condition.

Later, Dad and Jesse went swimming off the boat and I went below and took a snooze. (Will I ever feel 100 percent again?) We headed home right before sunset. Jesse and I sat on the bow of the boat and watched as it cut through the water like a knife. He slipped his hand over mine and it was like we were in perfect sync with each other, like we had one heart beating between us.

When we got home, Dad made ice cream and Jesse and I watched the fireflies come out. He said, "You want me to catch some in a jar for you?"

I said, "Sure."

And he said, "Did you know that scientists pay for these bugs? I catch them out where I live and stick them in the freezer. When I've got a bagful, I take them into the science department at the university and they pay me thirty-one cents a gram for them—nine dollars an ounce."

"They don't look like they weigh much," I said.

"It's a way to earn money," he said. "And I'm helping a scientific cause."

As usual, Jesse's knowledge surprised me, so I urged him to catch a hundred fireflies and stick them in our freezer, but when he brought the jar to me and I saw the flies trapped inside, their little lighted bodies going dim, I started to cry.

"What's wrong?" he said.

"It's sad," I said. "They don't hurt anyone. They're so gentle. And now scientists are going to experiment on them."

Jesse said, "They're insects. They have no nerve endings or higher brains."

I kept crying and said, "I don't care. It just doesn't seem fair that they should die."

Jesse said, "They don't have to die." Then he unscrewed the lid and let them all go.

I felt stupid because I'd made him throw away spending money. I said, "I'm sorry."

And he said, "I promise I will never catch fireflies again, because they should never be held against their will, or frozen and dissected, even if it is for the good of science."

I wondered if he was poking fun at me for being so silly about an insect, but when I looked into his beautiful blue eyes, I saw that he was serious. He'd held the power of life and death over them but had released them, allowing them to live on, to please me. And while we watched them fly off into the night, I got the feeling that we weren't really talking about fireflies at all, but about mercy and kindness and doing something nice just because you can.

September 7 (one of the worst and BEST days ever!)

We took Jesse to the airport today at noon. When we came home, I locked myself in my room and had a good cry. I'm going to miss him so much! I already feel like there's a big hole inside me because he's gone. I think he might like me too. (I hope.)

Here's exactly what happened. Mom dropped us off and went to park the car so that Jesse could check in. We waited in line together, and after Jesse checked in, we hung around the terminal, because we both knew that once he went through the metal detectors it was really goodbye. (Mom had told me she'd park and come inside to look for me at the check-in counters.) Jesse held my hand and I tried to act cheerful and not to cry even though there was a lump in my throat the size of a tennis ball.

He said, "I really had a good time."

I said, "Me too. Thanks for coming."

He said, "Can I come again someday?"

I said, "Will you? Maybe next summer. You think?"

He said, "Maybe."

A tear trickled down my cheek and he wiped it off. He said, "I'll e-mail and write. You too?"

All I could do was nod, because I didn't want to bawl like a baby.

He headed toward security to wait in line and pass through. The line was moving slowly, but not too slow for me, because I didn't want him to leave. He was almost at the front of the line when he turned and hurried back to me. I stared, wondering what was going on. He said, "I forgot something."

"What?" I asked.

Then he grabbed me and kissed me right on the mouth! Before I could react, he turned and raced back to security, threw his backpack on the conveyor belt, and went through the detectors without setting off any alarms. Except for the one inside my heart. It was ringing like crazy. Everyone around us was watching, and I know I must have turned twenty shades of red. Here I was, standing in Hartsfield Airport with hundreds of people heading off to their flights, and I, Melinda Skye, fourteen for only a week, had experienced my first real kiss in front of God and everybody.

Today, Jesse kissed me, fast and hard, and it felt wonderful. Best of all, he meant it with all his heart. Tomorrow, I'll tell Bailey. Tonight, it belongs to just me.

MELINDA'S DIARY

Friday the 13th

Chemo sucks. It took an hour and it hurt. The only thing that saved the day was visiting my old floor and saying hi to the kids. Keisha has gone home. But I saw three new faces of kids who've checked in since I left.

Cancer sucks too. Especially when it picks on little kids. I'm tired now and don't feel much like writing.

TO: All Concerned
Subject: Outpatient Chemo Begins

This has been a hard week for our little girl. Her friend Jesse Rose returned to California, she started homebound schooling, and her outpatient chemo treatments began. The protocols are two weeks on (three days a week) and one week off, for the next three months. Once chemo is over, she'll be tested frequently over the next six months and if she remains cancer-free, she'll return for semiannual checkups over the next few years. If the drugs do their part, she should be out of the woods in five years (by the time she's eighteen and heading off to college, this whole ordeal should just be a really bad memory).

I told her I'll take her to Paris to celebrate when her chemo treatments are over. She said, "Dad, save your money . . . I'm going with a dance troupe." What a girl! She never forgets her dreams and goals. Elana and I are so proud of her. Elana has dropped all her outside activities, except tennis, which she says she needs to "vent" and blow off stress. I use golf for the same purpose.

Thanks again for all your concerns. I'll only post if there's something meaningful to say.

Lenny and Elana

MELINDA'S DIARY

September 20

   Jesse wrote to say he really liked the B-day gift I sent (it's getting harder to think up good things to give him anymore—hey, maybe I'll mail him ME!). I keep thinking about him kissing me. I wish it could have been in private, because now I wonder if he did it just to say thanks for the good time, or if he meant it from his heart. I finally told Bailey how it happened and she said it was "really romantic," because he was almost through security and had to make a special effort to come back to kiss me. I tried to play it down because I know she's been kissed lots of times. And me? Well, who wants to kiss a girl with cancer except for a best friend, like Jesse? (Who may just feel sorry for me.)

He says he wants to come visit again next summer. I'd like that, IF I'm looking like my regular self and IF I don't have an invitation to dance school again.

Homebound school isn't too bad. I get the work done easily, but I miss going to school. I miss seeing friends in the halls, the smell of chalk dust and, yes, even the cafeteria food. Bailey (the nut!) took a video camera to school and made a tape for me she calls "A Day in the Life of . . ." She had that camera running all day. She interviewed our friends, teachers, even the principal. Everyone says they miss me and want me to hurry back. Some of the guys on the soccer team sing to me. Very cute (and very bad singers). I've watched it sooo many times. It makes me laugh. But it also makes me cry because I can't be there.

Elana's Journal

September 25

Now that life has settled more into a routine, I can be reflective of the past few months. What can I say? For so long, I was in "emergency mode"—sheer panic over what was happening to Melinda. Now I feel as if we're treading water. Our lives revolve around her chemo treatments and their aftermath. Some days she's too sick to even sit up. Others, she endures the treatment just fine. There's no predicting. As it drags on and I watch her push herself, I want to insist that she rest and take it easier. But it makes her angry if I meddle. It's dance that drives her.

Last week, we got caught in traffic and she became tense because she knew she was going to be late for class. (An unpardonable sin most of the time although Mrs. Houston has given Melinda great leeway with the studio "rules.") Still, Melinda holds herself to a high standard and refuses to "cave," as she calls it, to bend or break studio protocols. In short, she won't allow herself any special privileges no matter what.

Anyway, we got caught in traffic after chemo and by the time I pulled into the parking lot, she was extremely upset. She opened the car door and discreetly vomited. It broke my heart to see her heaving, knowing I could do nothing to help her. When she was finished, she dug out a bottle of mouthwash she keeps in her dance duffel bag and rinsed her mouth, took a few deep breaths and got out of the car. I said, "Honey, do you have to go?"

And she said, "Yes, I have to go."

I watched her toss her gear bag over her shoulder and march into the studio. I cried ... for her, for my helplessness, for all the things I can't change.

MELINDA'S DIARY

October 4

Mrs. Houston reminded us that Natalie Blackbird will arrive next week with some of the Denver dancers to begin rehearsals and to lead our advance class. So now I have a goal. Be in competitive shape for the experience AND get picked for a role in this season's Nutcracker. And boy, do I ever have a long way to go.

October 10

I found a few hairs growing on my body today! My eyebrows look as if they're coming back and maybe I can chuck the false eyelashes in another few weeks. Knowing how to put on stage makeup and fake hair and lashes has been a real plus. At least I don't look like a plucked chicken when I go to the trouble to paste it all on.

TO: Jesse
Subject: This and That

I hope you don't mind resuming our e-mail talks. I thought you'd like to hear about Melinda from an observer like me, one who cares about her as much as you do. (OK, maybe not in exactly the same way, but just as much in a best friend way.) She's really doing pretty good. The other day I went with her for a chemo treatment. She sat in this chair that looks like a big recliner and a nurse hung a bag of liquid, hooked it into the shunt in Melinda's chest and said she'd check on her in a bit.

I tell you, my eyes were riveted to that gizmo, and for a minute, I felt all queasy in my stomach. But Melinda never noticed. She said, "Let's play Scrabble," like it was the most ordinary thing in the world. So we played (she tromped me), then we watched some TV (each little private chemo room has an overhead TV). Finally, the nurse came back. The bag was empty, so she unhooked Melinda, took some vital signs and said, "See you in a couple of days."

Melinda looked pale, but she got up. We rode down in the elevator, met her mother in the lobby and drove home. M. just rested against the seat and listened to a CD while we maneuvered through traffic. Jesse, it was as if this was the most ordinary way to spend an afternoon instead of the most ghoulish. She's so brave!

B

TO: Bailey
Subject: Melinda

Thanks for writing to me. You're right—I only hear good stuff from M. Nothing bad. I know chemo is hard, because a woman in my mom's office is being treated for breast cancer and Mom's dropped some info about what a hard time the woman's having. So I figured M. can't be breezing through it like she sometimes pretends. It's really hard for me to be so far away while she's going through all this. I guess it's no secret that I care about her. Really care.

My school is having some dumb fall festival dance and a girl asked me to take her. Beth's nice, but I don't feel about her the way I feel about M. I decided to go to the dance, but I'll be thinking about M. the whole time. She's all I think about most of the time anyway.

Jesse

MELINDA'S DIARY

October 18

The nurse talked to me (again!) about joining the teen cancer support group. They meet on the second Friday of every month at seven o'clock in the hospital auditorium. I tried to be polite, but I have no intention of EVER going to those meetings. I don't want to hang around with a bunch of kids with cancer. I want to hang around with regular kids—kids who aren't sick, who've never been sick. Maybe that's selfish of me, but it's the way I feel. I WON'T GO!!!!!

TO: Ballerina Girl
Subject: Control

I don't blame you for not wanting to go to cancer support meetings. Mom suggested I go to a kids of divorced parents group that meets on her college campus, but I nixed that idea as soon as it was out of her mouth. Who wants to sit around with a bunch of strangers and dis their parents' divorce? Not me.

Dad's putting pressure on me to fly to NY for Christmas. That's not going to happen. What would Mom do? Spend the holiday alone! No way. She said it was all right with her if I went, but I could see by the look on her face she didn't mean it. I'm not bailing on her the way he did.

I won a blue ribbon in a skateboard competition last Saturday (Mom got me a new one for my

B-day—state-of-the-art, a fine piece of work-manship). I've lined up a job in a sporting equipment store for the Christmas break. Just a few hours a day, unloading stock and stocking shelves, but it's a paycheck.

Wish I could see you for Christmas.

Jesse

MELINDA'S DIARY

October 22

I'm sad tonight. Bailey let it drop that Jesse is going to a dance with some girl named Beth from his school. B. acted all embarrassed once she'd spilled the news. She said she was sorry, that she'd never meant for me to know. I'm not sure if I'm mad at her or not. It hurt because my feelings for Jesse are mixed up. But it's not fair for me to expect him never to look at another girl. Unrealistic too. He's more than a thousand miles from here. I guess I'm lucky he still thinks of me at all.

It would have been better if he'd never kissed me. I wish B. had kept her big mouth shut.

---------------   ❧   ---------------

MELINDA'S DIARY

November 15

Jesse's never said a word about the dance or the girl he took. I've pumped Bailey, but she swears he's never mentioned it to her in his e-mails either. She said she even asked, but he didn't answer. I asked her why they're e-mailing each other in the first place, and she said it's because she feels like they have a lot in common—me, of course, but also divorced parents. She says I can never understand what it's like to feel rejected and unwanted by a parent—which is different from Jesse's situation because both his parents want him. Still, Bailey thinks they're "kindred spirits."

Yikes! What's wrong with me? B. is my friend. And so is Jesse. The real problem is this girl, Beth. I wonder, is she pretty? Is she sexy? Whatever she is, I'm sure she doesn't have cancer. I'm so mixed up. I wish B. had never told me about Beth and Jesse! What was she thinking?

December 15

Chemo's over. I feel like a person let out of prison. They removed the shunt too and I'm sure not going to miss THAT sucker! I'm learning so much with Ms. Blackbird. She's worked individually with me and says I'm inspiring. She says I should audition for the Denver ballet group when I'm sixteen because they take young dancers for summer internships. I can't believe it! She thinks I'm good enough to become a part of her company's dance corps! Of course, if I'm accepted (fat chance!) and can really join a troupe full-time after graduation, I'll have to forgo college . . . at least for a while. I don't know how Mom and Dad would take the news. I know they have a college fund for me, and Grandma left me a chunk for college too. But dance supersedes college in my book! I won't be able to dance forever and I can always go to college.

Our Christmas performance will be at the Fox Theater Friday night. I've been dancing in The Nutcracker *since I was a kid, but I'm more excited about this one than I've ever been about others. Dad says we can buy a copy of the tape PBS is shooting of the performance and we'll send it to Jesse for a Christmas present. I wonder if he'll care (now that Beth is in the picture).*

TO: Bailey
Subject: Third Degree

Why do you keep asking about Beth in your e-mails? There is NO me and Beth. I took her to a dance because she asked me to. I have no plans to date her. She's OK, but not right for me. Please don't ever tell Melinda about Beth. I don't want her to think any girl means more to me than she does. And that's the truth. Thanks for keeping my secret (which I never should have dumped on you).

Jesse

MELINDA'S DIARY

December 20

I spent the evening consoling Bailey because Kerry broke up with her. He's such a RAT! He dumped her right before Christmas—probably because he's too cheap to buy her a gift! I reminded her that he'd done the same thing to Allison and she's pregnant! I think B. knows deep down she's better off without him. According to B. he was mak-

ing too many demands on her anyway. I can guess what "demands" she means too.

It's hard for her, though, because she's the kind of girl who always thinks she needs a guy. I've never been able to figure out why. She's a great person, fun to be with, always ready to do anything for a friend. I wish she could see herself through my eyes.

I realize she's a little bit of a drama queen too. She tends to blow everything way out of proportion until it takes on gigantic importance. Good thing she wasn't the one who got leukemia. How would she have coped with that?

"Merry Christmas, Melinda."

"Jesse? Is this really you?"

"No . . . it's my evil twin. Just kidding. . . . How are you?"

"I—I'm fine. And you?"

"Fine. Listen, I called to thank you for the tape. And the Braves shirt. They're both perfect."

"You're welcome. . . . Thanks for the rose pendant. I'm wearing it now."

"I'm glad you like it. The tape is my favorite thing. You look so . . . so real. I've replayed the Chinese dance part so many times I can hum the music in my sleep."

"Tchaikovsky would be pleased to know that."

"You, um . . . looked beautiful. Even prettier than that famous ballerina you like so much."

"I don't think so, but thanks for saying it. So . . . what did you get for Christmas?"

"My father sent a video camera. Said that if I won't come to him, then the least I can do is send tapes of my day-to-day life. It's a pretty good idea, actually. I can send you tapes too."

"Would you?"

"I've taped our apartment and me and Mom opening presents this morning."

"How's your mom? We didn't get a Christmas letter from her this year."

"She's all right. Wrung out because she's taking an extra course this term. So tell me, is everything still okay with you?"

"I guess so. My latest blood counts were normal. I'm going back to school in January. You know—back into the classroom. I'm excited, but sort of scared about it too."

"Why?"

"I've been out ever since last May. Everybody's so far ahead of me. Not with studies and class work, but with friends and cliques and all the social stuff. Know what I mean?"

"Bailey's there. She'll make sure you fit right in, won't she?"

"She'll help, but I may be a total social retard. I'll have to see how the kids treat me."

"You didn't plan on getting cancer. They should be nice to you."

"We'll see, won't we?"

> **<Melinda>** When Jesse and I talked, I really wanted to ask him about Beth.
>
> **<Bailey>** You didn't, did you!?!
>
> **<Melinda>** No. I bailed. Lost my nerve.
>
> **<Bailey>** Whew! So glad you didn't, because I wasn't supposed to tell you about her. If he finds out I did, he'll never tell me anything again!
>
> **<Melinda>** Then I'm doubly glad I didn't. He tells you things he

doesn't tell me. It hurts my
feelings.

<Bailey> Back up, girlfriend.
Why would he tell you about
another girl? Poor strategy.

<Melinda> Do you think he
really likes Beth but is only
being nice to me for old time's
sake?

<Bailey> NO WAY!!! He's not a
jerk like Kerry who's telling
everybody that he and I did IT
(which is a total lie, if anyone
says anything to you. Sure he
pressured me, but I held him off
and now am I ever glad I did!). I
can't wait until high school.
Maybe the guys will be more
mature.

<Melinda> News flash,
Bailey . . . you've already dated
high school guys and didn't like
the way they treated you.

<Bailey> So maybe I won't date anybody. Most guys are jerks anyway.

<Melinda> Bailey without a boyfriend? I won't believe it until I see it. Not to change the subject (OK, changing the subject), want to come over New Year's Eve and stay up with me and watch the ball drop in Times Square on TV? I'm going to call Jesse and say happy New Year at midnight. You can wish him the same thing.

<Bailey> New Year's Eve sounds fine. Patti's having a party, but I don't want to go because Kerry's going to be there with his new airhead girlfriend. Who wants to be subjected to seeing them do the kissy-face thing all night long? Not me! And yes, I'd like wishing Jesse happy New Year. You know, he may be the only nice guy left on the planet.

<Melinda> Bring brownies, the ones you bake with the M&M's in them. I'll cover the popcorn and soda. We'll have fun. And Jesse will be so surprised. Yikes! I just thought of something. What if he's at a party with Beth?

<Bailey> Then he'll hate himself because he wasn't home when you called. Trust me.

December 30

My Confession

    I am pond scum. Puppy piddle. Turtle turds and beetle dung. And every other nasty thing I can think of! Why am I all of these loathsome things? Because I've fallen in love with Jesse Rose. And the only reason I'm writing it down is that there's no one I can tell. Especially my best friend in the whole entire world, Melinda. And if I don't tell someone, I'm going to burst. So this piece of notebook paper becomes my "confessor" and the keeper of my awful secret.

    Jesse treats Melinda like she's a queen. I want a guy to treat me the same way. But no boy does. Things start out good between us, but once we get used to each other and the goo-goo feelings fade, we drift apart. Most of the time, I get pressured to do things I don't want to do with the guy. If I don't cave, he walks. That's the way it was with Kerry.

Except I did let him go a little too far (not all the way, but almost!). So now he's spreading rumors, and there's nothing I can do, because kids at school want to believe him—Mr. Cool Jock. Now other guys are asking me out because they think I'm easy—which I'm NOT!

I never want Melinda to know any of this. Especially how I feel about Jesse. What kind of friend wants her best friend's guy? Especially a best friend who's sick with a terrible disease? Also, I know the truth about Jesse and Beth (that Beth is nothing to him) and I don't tell Melinda. Still I let Melinda think the worst.

See how worthless I am? I hate me. But not enough to stop loving Jesse.

Signed,
Bailey Taylor
Prisoner of Dark Secrets

P.S. I feel better after writing this. Tomorrow night I'll hear Jesse's voice on the phone. It'll break my heart *because I know he only cares for Melinda, but I want to hear him so much. Love hurts. Oh yeah . . . it hurts big-time.*

———————— ❧ ————————

MELINDA'S DIARY

January 3

Returned to school today. Scared, but happy to be back. I'd forgotten how loud the halls can be after all the time I've spent alone at home. I stood at my locker and soaked up the atmosphere like a sponge. Some kid almost ran into me and I nearly panicked because I sure don't want to get injured and end up back in the hospital. I've had enough of hospitals to last me the rest of my life!

In homeroom, everybody was friendly, but I knew they were talking about me. "She's the girl with cancer," a girl whispered (loud enough for me to hear). "Is she bald?" "Is she wearing a wig?" others asked. I wanted to yell "No," but I wasn't supposed to hear them, so I kept my mouth shut and kept smiling. Don't they know it hurts to be talked about? What's wrong with people anyway?

Mom got permission from the superintendent of schools for me to carry a pager at school. If I ever get sick, I can page her and she can come get me. But I won't use it because it's so lame, and besides, it makes me feel even more like an outsider. I ate lunch with Bailey (lucky we have the same schedule!) and got eyeballed by the football players. Bailey says that they're shunning her. Why is Kerry being so mean to her? I'm glad I know someone like Jesse, who's never been mean to me.

P.S. I think he's over Beth, because on New Year's Eve, he said he was sitting alone by the phone wishing he could hear my voice. If Beth were really important to him, he'd have been with her. That's what I think, anyway.

February 14

Jesse is so cute and original! He sent me a beautiful bouquet of flowers for my desk for Valentine's Day. My desktop on my computer, that is. His virtual roses arrived in this morning's e-mail and I've had them up and running since I got home from school. I can change their color and their size whenever I want. I put them right in the middle of my screen and every time I look at them, I smile. He makes me so happy!

February 14

Dear Self,

This is the first Valentine's Day that I haven't had a boyfriend since I can remember. No matter. Jesse's the only boy I like. And I know he'll never like me in the same way.

Maybe I'll become a nun.

(Sister) Bailey

May 23

Dear Lenny and Elana,

No, you're not seeing things. There really is a graduation announcement enclosed in this envelope. Isn't it beautiful? I never thought this day would come, but I graduate from the Santa Cruz College School of Education on Friday. I can hardly believe it myself! I've even impressed Jesse—which is a hard thing for the mother of a teenage boy to do, don't you know! I only wish you all could attend the ceremony and share my happiness.

Now comes the challenge of finding a job. I've sent out résumés to high schools throughout the area and already have four interviews scheduled. Jesse wants us to return to Atlanta, of course. Naturally, I know why. He's still smitten with Melinda, even after all these years. Goodness knows I've tried to make a life for the two of us here, but he still yearns for what he can't have. I've told him that he can apply to any college he wants, and frankly his grades are good enough that I know he'll qualify for scholarship money somewhere. He tells me he wants to study medicine. Can you imagine? My son, the doctor!

Thank you for your encouragement over the years. Friends like you are few and far between.

Ann

TO: Melinda
Subject: Summer Vacation

There's no getting out of it. I have to spend most of the summer with my dad in New York. Mom and I had a fight about it, but she says her hands are tied, there's nothing she can do to keep me from having to go. She says I have to do what he says until I'm eighteen. It sucks.

Jesse

\<Melinda> I was online when your e-mail arrived, so don't go away.

\<Jessie> Hey! Why are you up so late?

\<Melinda> Term paper due tomorrow and I'm behind. I'm feeling tired and I crash as soon as I get home instead of getting right to my work. 'Nuff about me. Sorry about your messed-up summer, but you just might have a good time. It wasn't nearly as bad as you thought it would be last time you went. Remember?

\<Jessie> But I only had to stay a few weeks last time. This is for the whole summer. What will you be doing?

\<Melinda> Dad surprised me and Mom with plans for a six-week vacation to Europe. We leave on June 11. I was

planning on taking extra dance
classes this summer (since I
missed out on Washington this
year), but that's out now. I've
always wanted to see Europe.
Of course, I thought it would be
with a dance troupe instead of
with Mom and Dad, but Dad
made me a promise when I was
in the hospital.

<Jessie> Your dad's the best!
Will you have e-mail?

<Melinda> Yes . . . Dad's taking
his laptop. Give me your New
York snail mail and e-mail
addresses, and I'll keep in
touch. Well, I've got to get back
to my paper, but it's been really
nice talking to you.

<Jessie> It sure has! I wish I
could see you this summer. Even
though my visit last summer
wasn't under the best conditions,
at least I got to see you. Just

**wait until I'm eighteen . . . I'm
moving to Atlanta.**

<Melinda> I'll hold you to that!

June 25

*Hello, dear Melinda. I hope this finds you well
and happy. I am writing you this brief note because
I wanted to tell you that I have spoken to our director, Jeremy McAllister, about your considerable talent. He is most curious to see your audition videos,
so when you can, please send your tape to the address on the front of this envelope, to my attention. I
will see to it that Jeremy views it immediately. Who
knows, perhaps he will offer you a summer apprenticeship!*

*As you well know, the world of ballet is most com-
petitive, and with companies folding continually
for lack of funding, spots in a good company are
difficult to earn. However, I do believe you have a
chance of achieving your goals. Work hard this
summer, and I'll look for your package for Jeremy.*

Ciao,
Natalie Blackbird

———————— ❧ ————————

Dear Jesse,

Paris is awesome. So far, we've visited the Eiffel Tower, Notre Dame, the Arc de Triomphe, lots of shops and two art museums—the Musée du Louvre and Musée d'Orsay. Just walking through the galleries made me feel a part of history. When I saw the Mona Lisa, I got goose bumps, but when I saw some of the original Degas ballerina series, I cried. The paintings seem to glow and the dancers look as if they might stand or turn or smile at any moment. I was surrounded by the ghosts of greatness and long-dead images of once-living people. It was eerie.

M

Hey Bailey,

You would absolutely LOVE Paris! A paradise for a fashion diva like you. The teens are très chic like nothing I've ever seen before. I look so totally frumpy by comparison. Biggest turnoff for me is that they all smoke. I'm not kidding; kids 11 and 12 years old stand at bus stops with cigarettes, puffing away. Ugh. And little motor scooters dart around with girls holding on to some guy who's driving. No helmet laws either. I bought you a present at the cutest little boutique (the salesgirl said Madonna shops there). You must come to Paris someday (maybe to visit me when I dance here one day in the future!).

Hugs, M

Jesse,
   Arrived in Madrid yesterday. Today it rained and we spent the day at the Prado. More art treasures to see. I guess this might be boring to most American teens, but not to me. Dragging around with my parents can be a bore—honestly, they are so CONSTANT—but still I'm having a good time. It would be more fun if you and Bailey were along on the trip, but I can't have everything. Hope you're surviving your stay in New York.

M

   P.S. Will try for e-mail hookup 8 P.M., July 4 (six-hour time difference should catch you at 2 P.M.).

<Melinda> Are you there?

<Jessie> You bet! Didn't get your postcard until yesterday though.

<Melinda> I mailed it ten days ago! Talk about s-l-o-w. . . . What's going on?

<Jessie> Fireworks tonight at Shea Stadium after Mets game. How about you?

<Melinda> We've toured most of Spain. Loved Granada and Seville best. No fireworks here because no one cares that it's America's birthday. It's funny being in a foreign country for one of our holidays. Anyway, last 4th I was in D.C., and my troubles began. Hard to believe it's been a year since my diagnosis. Sure glad it's all behind me.

<Jessie> Me too. Where are you headed next?

<Melinda> We leave for Germany tomorrow and then we'll take a tour of what Dad calls "the blond countries" (cute, huh?) . . . you know, Sweden, Holland, Denmark. I'm having fun, but I'm getting homesick.

<Jessie> I guess you're not dancing.

<Melinda> No. And I feel stiff and fat from nonmovement. Oh, before I forget, today's Bailey's birthday. I sent her an electronic card, but it would be nice if you e-mailed her and wished her a happy birthday. OK?

<Jessie> Will do. When will you be home?

<Melinda> August 1. Europe's nice, but there's no place like home. (Didn't someone named Dorothy say that?)

<Jessie> It depends on where your home is, I guess. Mine is definitely not in New York! Keep writing. Your postcards keep me going.

MELINDA'S DIARY

August 3

I'm glad to be home, but I'm so jet-lagged that I haven't even unpacked. While we were away, Dad had a gazebo built in our backyard as a surprise for Mom. She's always wanted one and it is really cool. I'm looking out my bedroom window and seeing her sitting there with her morning coffee and the newspaper. The lawn service planted vines around the base, and by next summer, it'll be covered with flowers. It'll be so romantic!

Bailey loved her B-day gift from Paris and had a fit over the things I brought back from all the countries we visited. My big project before school starts will be a scrapbook full of photos and ticket stubs and programs. I'll call it "Europe on $500 a Day," which Dad thinks is very funny (and accurate, according to Mom, because Dad spared no expense!).

Bailey has gone all summer without a boyfriend—some kind of record for her, I think. She says she's not hooking up with any guy who doesn't treat her good (the way Jesse treats me, she says). She told me he sent her a B-day e-mail, but she seemed kind of disappointed when I told her I'd suggested it to him. Probably my imagination.

Back to the studio on Saturday, and boy am I ever rusty. Sooo glad I have the mini-studio in the garage to work out my kinks before Mrs. Houston sees me. But I am looking like my old self again. All hair has made a complete comeback. Weight's gone. Boobs no bigger. Oh well. . . . Two out of three ain't bad.

August 3 (night)

Mom sorted through stacks of mail held at the post office and gave me the note from Natalie Blackbird. I almost fainted! And I can't believe it arrived just AFTER we had left on vacation. What bad timing! Anyway, we'll get a package together tomorrow and send it off FedEx. Mom said she'd write a note explaining why it took so long for us to respond. I hope the delay won't count against me!

TO: Ballerina Girl
Subject: Can I Visit?

You'll never believe what my dad says he'll do for me. He's willing to route my return trip to California through Atlanta with a weekend stay-over if it's okay with your parents. All your postcards and e-mails made him curious about you (yes, he does remember you from our first-grade class and the night of the *Nutcracker* performance), and he was surprised that we've kept in touch all this time.

I told him about you and how I stayed with your family so much right after his and Mom's divorce, and about how I used to wish your dad was MY dad. I really dumped on him. He got all teary, almost broke down, said it had been hard on him too with Mom moving to California and him not being able to watch me grow up. He said he was sorry, that divorce is always hard, but that his and Mom's marriage hadn't been good from the start. I told him I didn't want him dissing Mom and he didn't. He just said, "The past is the past. We all made mistakes." He said he only wants to start fresh with me because he loves me.

Anyway, we cleared the air and I guess I can see both sides of their divorce now. Donna and Dad get along real well and I can tell it makes a difference when two people really care for each other. Then he offered to route me through Atlanta to visit you. I really want to come. Can I? I promise not to be a bother. I want to see you again.

Jesse

TO: Jesse
Subject: Your Trip

Yes, you can come! I'll be at the airport to meet your flight. And this time, Mom promises not to talk!

M

August 17

    This is one of the worst nights of my life. I look across the street and see a light glowing on Melinda's porch and I know she's outside in her yard in the gazebo with Jesse. She told me she was making them a picnic supper and they were going to "dine under the stars." I acted excited and even helped her pick out music for her CD player and candles for her big evening with him. But inside, my heart was breaking. I want to be the one with Jesse under the stars. I want him to hold me and kiss me.

    But she's my best friend and I could never make a move for him. It would be traitorous. Plus, I know the truth: Jesse loves Melinda. Therefore, he'll never love me. If only I could find a guy like Jesse. If only my brain would turn off and I could stop thinking about them and feeling sorry for myself. If only I could give up this impossible dream. If only . . .

MELINDA'S DIARY

August 17

Years from now, when I think of this night, I will count it as one of the best of my life. And for the first time ever, my dream of becoming a professional ballerina slipped into the background. Why? Because tonight Jesse kissed me. Not the quick kiss-and-run of last summer, but a real kiss, one that left my knees shaky and my heart racing.

I can still taste the peppermint of his tongue and smell the lemony scent of his skin. I can still feel the warmth of his body and the touch of his hands on my arms and around my waist. I can hardly hold the pen straight as I write this. But I will try to write it down just as it happened, so that I will never forget what it felt like. . . .

In the afternoon, Jesse played at my computer and swore not to peek while Bailey and I got things ready for a special backyard picnic for me and Jesse. Bailey helped me pack a basket and choose special music. We made chicken salad and cut up some watermelon. "And here is a bag of M&M's," Bailey said before shutting the lid of the hamper basket.

"You look sad," I said to her. I had noticed that

she'd been awfully quiet while we worked—not typical for Bailey.

"No," she said. "Just green with envy."

"You'll find the right guy this year," I told her.

"Maybe," she said, looking like she was going to cry.

"For sure," I said.

Maybe I should have been a better friend and pressed her to tell me why she was so sad, but I didn't because all I could think about was my evening with Jesse. (I'll make it up to her after he leaves.)

After the food was ready, Bailey helped me spread a blanket on the floor of the gazebo and place big squishy cushions all around. We set thirty-six votive candles on the railings and Mom's silver candelabra on a tray in the center of the blanket. I put my CD player on a bench.

"It looks beautiful," I said to Bailey.

"Yes," she said. "Like a fairyland."

"You think?" I said.

"You're so lucky," she said, and hugged me, then jogged away before I could even say thank you. Strange.

Mom and Dad went to dinner and a movie (very nice of them) and later, when the stars came out, Jesse and I walked together from the house to the gazebo. He carried the picnic basket and at the gazebo he stood for a minute looking at all the flickering candles (which I'd lit minutes before), and he said, "You did all this for me?"

"For both of us," I told him. "Do you like it?"

"I like it," he said. "Very much."

We ate and talked and told each other our life plans. We've been friends for years, and I know a lot about him, but not everything. He told me that he really does want to become a doctor and I asked, "Since when?"

"Since you got sick," he said. "I want to make people well. Especially kids."

"It takes a long time to become a doctor," I said.

"I don't care how long it takes," he said. "It's what I want to do."

After a while, we didn't say anything; he just leaned against the big cushions and pulled me to his side and we gazed through the candles at the stars. There was no moon, just a million stars winking down at us and a CD playing Clair de Lune. Jesse nuzzled my ear and whispered, "I love you, Melinda."

I turned my face toward him and his lips touched mine and it was like a rocket went off inside my head and my heart. I said, "I love you too, Jesse," because I really, really DO love him. I asked,

"When did you know it?" (Because I was curious about how friendship turned into love for him when we live so far apart and he has another life way out in California.)

He said, "Maybe on the first day of school in first grade, when I saw you standing in the doorway. I remember you were dressed in a yellow dress. You looked like sunshine and you lit up all the dark places inside me."

I laughed and told Jesse that he had quite a memory. Grandma had given the dress to me along with shiny yellow patent leather shoes.

He said, "I thought you were a princess." Then he looked into my eyes, and my heart picked up speed again. "My happiest memories are of those afternoons when I came to your house and we played together," he said. "Even when I fell out of the tree and broke my arm, I was happy, because it meant I could stay at your place and I didn't have to listen to my parents fight."

I felt sad for him. And happy that our family had given him a place to belong.

Jesse reached into his pocket, dropped something small into my hand and closed my hand around it. He said, "Will you take this? It's a birthday present, but I want to give it to you now. I bought it in New York before I came."

"What is it?" I asked before I opened my hand.

"A birthstone ring," he said. "But it's also a promise ring, because I want you to promise that someday you'll take a real ring from me and wear it forever."

I held the ring up and the green stone twinkled— almost as if it was winking at me. I put the ring on my finger and started crying. Jesse kissed me again. And then again. And again. And again. Within the gazebo it was as if we were the only two people in the universe and the stars had left the sky and rained their fire into my heart.

I belong to Jesse and he belongs to me. He leaves tomorrow. How will I ever get through the rest of the year without him to hold me?

September 25

Dear Melinda,

I've decided to start writing letters to you because I might want to say something that's too personal for e-mail that anyone might be able to read. (You know who I mean—parents!) I'll also keep up the e-mail, but today it's a letter, because I haven't stopped thinking about our time under the stars. Next summer, I'm coming to Atlanta if I have to hitchhike all the way. I can get a job there just as easily as here. And Dad will just have to understand any cutback on my visit to NY so that I can spend more time with you. I don't know where I'll stay, or how I'll manage all the details, but I'm coming. So be prepared.

I love you and I want to be with you. Nothing's going to get in my way.

Forever yours,
Jesse

P.S. Mom is substitute teaching but will take over for a middle-school teacher going on maternity leave in January. She thinks it will lead to a full-time position, which means she'll never leave California. But I will.

October 1

Dear Jesse,

I loved getting a letter from you and I've tied it up with a red ribbon and stashed it in my memory box (along with your other notes and cards from first grade till now). I hope you don't think this is silly—the memory box, I mean. It holds all my most treasured possessions, and your correspondence ranks right at the top of my favorite-things list. So there!

Having you around all summer would be a dream come true. My mind keeps playing back the night of our picnic like a videotape (except unlike a tape, it doesn't wear out). I will never forget a single minute of that night. Never! In class, I find myself staring down at my ring instead of listening to my teacher. It's like I share a secret with the ring. The ring knows and I know that you and I love each other. I haven't even told Bailey anything more than that we had a good time.

And speaking of Bailey, she still hasn't found a special guy. I feel sorry for her (which is another reason I don't talk to her much about us. I don't want her to think, "Melinda has a boyfriend and I don't and she's rubbing it in." Know what I mean?).

Keep writing. I miss you every minute.

Love always,
Melinda

Hey M

   Here I am in study hall with time dragging. Thank God Christmas break starts on Monday. I'd love to go with you and watch you dance in The Nutcracker this Friday. Thanks for asking me, but please don't think I'm a charity case just because I don't have anyone in my life like you do. After my bad experience with Kerry, I've reevaluated myself and decided that until I can have something as special as you do with Jesse, I'd rather have nothing with anyone. Don't be shocked. . . . I know what I'm saying.

   Any word on your dance internship for next summer? What will you do about Jesse coming if you get an invite to Denver?

Bailey

B—

   I don't know. I want both—Jesse and a dance apprenticeship. First I have to see if Jesse can really stay and work in Atlanta, which will help me decide about the other. I've heard nothing from Denver, so I guess my audition tape and the influence of Ms. Blackbird wasn't enough. It was a long shot anyway.

Oh . . . don't come over after school. I feel like I'm coming down with the flu. Wouldn't you know it? Just when the holidays are coming. Oh, about Saturday, let's hit the mall early. I want you to help me pick out the perfect Christmas gift for Jesse. Two heads are better than one and I need to get it in the mail ASAP.

Thanks for being my friend. I don't know who I'd talk to if it weren't you!

Hugs . . . M

MELINDA'S DIARY

December 25

Christmas Day and it actually snowed in Atlanta! One whole inch! Bailey and I made pathetic little snowballs and threw them at each other. The snow was wet and sloppy and it hurt when it hit. I have a huge bruise on my arm and another on my leg, but one of my snowballs hit poor B. right in the face. I hope she doesn't bruise like I did.

Jesse called and hearing his voice was like magic. I miss him so much. He sent me a charm bracelet with a single gold rose on it. I told him I'd never put a charm on it that didn't come from him, and he laughed and said that we both may be graduating from high school before he can afford to add another.

Bailey's Diary

December 25

Melinda gave me this for Christmas and so I feel obligated to write in it. I'm not like her, though, and I can't imagine keeping this up every day like she does. But she's my friend and I said I'd give it a try. Besides, it's cute, with drawings of dresses and shoes on the cover.

Melinda showed me her charm bracelet from Jesse and I said it was beautiful, because it is. Jesse loves Melinda and she loves him. End of story. But I have to say that taking a vacation from having a boyfriend has helped me see some things. So far, I've picked a lot of losers. But no more! Here's my New Year's resolution: When classes begin, I'm going to look more closely at the less high-profile guys (the ones who aren't so cocky and stuck on themselves. Guys who are NICE to me).

I guess this is it for my first entry (and maybe my last). EOM (end of message). I saw that in a movie once.

MELINDA'S DIARY

March 17

I feel punky today. Too tired to write. Performed horribly in dance class. Got a C on a history test and shouldn't have. Just an all-around bad day.

March 30

I have to go for a bone marrow aspiration. Geez, I hate them so much!!!!! But Mom dragged me to our family doc, who did a blood test and said my white count's up (which totally freaked Mom, because it could signal the end of remission). He said I could just have a cold or maybe mono (it's going around at school) but that I should get another aspiration just to make sure. Easy for him to prescribe. He doesn't have to have one. So no dance class. Half day at the hospital. This really stinks!

The Denver Dance Theater

April 4

The Denver Dance Theater
1234 Yates Drive
Denver, CO 80202

Dear Ms. Skye:

After carefully reviewing your dance tape and your credentials along with the strong verbal recommendation of Natalie Blackbird, I am pleased to offer you a summer apprenticeship with the Denver Dance Company. Your expenses to Denver will be paid, along with room and board for the summer, plus compensation for your performances.

If this is satisfactory, a contract will follow for

you to sign and return, as well as a complete schedule of performances. Congratulations! We look forward to working with you as a member of our dance corps.

Sincerely,

Jeremy McAllister
Director
Denver Dance Company

MELINDA'S DIARY

April 4

Long horrible day at hospital, seeing doctors and getting needles shoved in me. I'd almost forgotten the horrors of chemo, but they all came back today. It's only been a little more than a year since I went through this. Thought the day was going to be a bust. Then the letter from Denver came and I about fainted. THEY WANT ME!!! I can't believe it. A whole summer as a professional dancer. Mom looked dazed and said we should wait until Dad's back home before we "firm up any plans."

Now that I've had time to think, I'm feeling very mixed up. Just when I thought Jesse and I might spend the summer together, the letter came. I want to do both—spend the summer with Jesse AND dance with the Denver company.

I took a time-out because Bailey called, and I told her what had happened. She said Jesse's plans weren't set in stone and I should tell him about the offer because she was betting that Jesse, being Jesse, would tell me to take the dance offer.

This just isn't fair! I've wanted to be a dancer all my life, but now I want other things too. Why does it all have to be so complicated? Whatever happened to a straight course? I can't imagine not dancing. But now I can no longer imagine my life without Jesse either. I love him so. . . . What am I going to do?

UNIVERSITY PATHOLOGY
CONSULTANTS
___

121 East 18th Street, Suite 318
Atlanta, GA 30020
Phone: (800) 555-4567 Fax: (800) 555-4568

___

BONE MARROW PATHOLOGY REPORT

Referring Physician: Janet Powell, M.D.
Specimen Number: JL01-99438
Hematology Associates

Emory University Hospital, Suite 2010
Atlanta, GA 30020

Date Collected: 4/04
Date Received: 4/04
Date Reported: 4/05

Diagnosis: Acute Lymphoblastic Leukemia

Gross Description
The specimen consists of 6 slides and 3 additional aliquots of 3 cc each, labeled "Bone Marrow Aspirate, Melinda Skye."

Microscopic Description:
The bone marrow aspirate demonstrates extensive hypercellularity with normal bone marrow elements essentially replaced by infiltrating lymphoblasts. There are multiple mitotic figures seen. The lymphoblasts demonstrate a high nuclear/cytoplasm ratio and clumped nuclear chromatin. Some nuclei display a folded appearance. Scattered among the abnormal cells are small numbers of erythroid, myeloid, and megakaryocytic cells.

Flow cytometric immunophenotypic studies demonstrated a population of beta lymphocytes, which expressed the CD19 and CD20 antigens.

Cytochemistry was positive for TdT, further corroborating a lymphoblastic process. The findings represent a relapse of acute lymphoblastic leukemia in this patient. **Prognosis poor, after so brief a remission.**

Stephen R. Jones, M.D.
Pathologist

Fallen Petals

I cried when I heard your news. I know it isn't macho, but I couldn't help it. Later, I went to the tennis courts and pounded the fuzz off a ball on the backboards. I hit the ball until I couldn't lift my arm and then I smashed the racket on the concrete. It didn't help. I'm still angry.

It's not fair that you're still fighting leukemia and that you have to go through chemo all over again. I'll call you so we can talk.

Jesse

TO: All Concerned
Subject: Melinda

This is one message I never wanted to write. According to Melinda's doctor, our daughter's cancer has returned. Apparently when this kind of leukemia recurs after such a brief remission, chances for another remission aren't so good. She begins a new round of chemo, but the magic drug they used before can't be used a second time. It's too toxic. What do they consider uncontrolled leukemia?

We ask you once again to keep our daughter in your thoughts and prayers. We'll keep you posted.

Lenny & Elana

═══════════════════════════

Elana's Journal

April 10

I'm out of the habit of writing in this thing.... I got lazy, confident I'd not need to write in it. But now I turn to pouring out my feelings here once more because I am confused and, yes, angry too. We did exactly as we were told. Melinda endured months of chemo, but now it seems that those months were for nothing. Her disease has returned, and this time her doctors don't act enthusiastic about her recovery. I'm smarter now. Before, I accepted all they said with a child's innocence. Now I know that medicine does not have all the answers. I know that doctors are not gods and that victims aren't just statistics.

Her doctors don't always look me in the eye when we talk. I think it's because they've thrown everything they have in their arsenal of drugs and potions at Melinda, and they've come to discover that her cancer is still stronger than their chemical weapons.

Lenny and I feel helpless. We watch her go through the same courses of drugs again. They didn't work before. Why would they work now? We have not yet told Melinda about the grimness, because she's struggling hard to endure the course. I can't rob her of hope. Neither can I consider the alternative.

MELINDA'S DIARY

April 25

I feel like I'm locked in a time warp. Didn't I just go through all this torture? I really thought it was over, but it isn't. The doctors come at me with terrible drugs that make me so sick. Stronger doses and longer treatments. And this time, I have to stay in the hospital 24/7. Still, my enemy doesn't retreat.

I've given up school. Too sick to even think about dance and the Denver offer. A dream come true and I'm too sick to consider it. Mom says I can make up

school this summer, but that would mean not dancing in Denver.

Sometimes I think Mom and Dad are keeping secrets from me. What could be more terrible than
this? If it wasn't for Jesse's constant e-mails, I would
go insane.

Bailey's Diary

April 27

*I think it's my fault that Melinda's sick again. I've
wished so hard and long for Jesse to be mine that the dark
side of the universe heard my secret thoughts and allowed
her sickness to return. Now I'm begging for her to get
well and never be struck with cancer again. I have given
up my hopeless love for Jesse (cross my heart). I would
give up anything else I have if only she would get well.
Please, please, let Melinda be all right.*

May 3

We miss you, dear Melinda. The class is less lively, less competitive without your spirit of excellence to spur us on. Please know that we think of you every day and that all your friends and classmates look forward to your return to health and our studio. Keep up the fight. We're on the sidelines cheering for you.

All your friends at the Atlanta School of Ballet

May 15

After speaking with your mother tonight, I know you will not be coming to Denver next month. I am sad for you, for your family, for our dance company, and for the world of ballet. But once you have beaten this monster, tell me and you will have another opportunity at an apprenticeship. I promise this. Your talent is pure and bright, and on the stage of life, you shine like a star.

With affection,
Natalie Blackbird

Elana's Journal

May 25

Dr. Neely brought Lenny and me into his office today to say what we already know. Nothing is working for Melinda. "What now?" Lenny asked.

"A bone marrow transplant may be her only hope," Dr. Neely said.

"Tell us more," I said.

And he did. He said that the best transplants are usually between siblings, but that because Melinda has no brother or sister, a parent could be considered. He suggested that both Lenny and I be tested to determine who would be the best donor. Naturally, Lenny and I agreed to be tested immediately.

But Dr. Neely also warned us that the procedure is risky, especially in Melinda's weakened condition. He told us that her immune system must be totally destroyed, leaving her vulnerable to even the normally most harmless germs, but that unless her immune system is taken out, her body will reject the transplant automatically. Even if the new bone marrow takes hold, she will have to take anti-rejection medications for the rest of her life. In short, there is great risk in this procedure, but he feels it is our daughter's only chance.

We have not told Melinda yet about the transplant possibility. Lenny is withdrawn and remote, and we are both frightened by our choices. Destroying Melinda's immune system is a huge risk. Yet not doing the transplant seems to be a bigger one. How can we gamble with our daughter's life?

MELINDA'S DIARY

June 1

How much longer am I going to be stuck in this hospital? I feel like an animal in a cage. I want out. I want to go home.

June 3

Jesse called again and just hearing his voice made me feel better. He said he's got a job bagging groceries six days a week because he wants to save up all the money he can. I thought about his plans to come to Atlanta this summer. I think about a lot of things these days. I have nothing else to do. I can't concentrate on reading books, and daytime TV is pathetic. I'm the only person my age up here, so there's no one to talk to except Mom. Sometimes Bailey comes, but I know she wishes she wasn't here. I can't blame her. I wish I wasn't here either.

Elana's Journal

June 3

Blood work results came back and it looks as if I'm the better match for the transplant. I want to tell Melinda, but Lenny says to wait until he returns from Europe, because he has something to talk about. I'm relieved about the test and for the first time in months, I feel hopeful. If my marrow takes, then Melinda really can be cancer-free.

June 6

Lenny and I had the worst fight we've ever had. While in Geneva, he looked into a special cancer clinic where extreme cases of the disease are treated. He talked with the head of the facility and now wants to transfer Melinda to Switzerland. I'm horrified. How can he even consider such a thing? I don't want our child treated by potential charlatans and quacks with hocus-pocus herbs and questionable medical procedures.

"And this way is better?" he shouted.

"Bone marrow transplants are proven cures," I shouted back.

"If she doesn't die getting the treatment," he yelled.

We stood staring at each other because that's the first time either of us had used that word in a sentence: DIE. Melinda might DIE.

MELINDA'S DIARY

June 6

Something's going on between Mom and Dad. Something bad. They hardly speak to each other and I can cut the tension with a knife when they're in the room together. This is my fault. They're having problems because of me and I don't know what to do about it.

I told Jesse and he said he thinks my family's one of the strongest he's ever known and I'm worrying for nothing. I hope he's right.

Elana's Journal

June 7

Dr. Neely is negative about the clinic idea, because he feels that it's the wrong choice medically. I told Lenny that Melinda must be told of her options—the transplant or the European clinic. Lenny wants us to decide, because Melinda's still a minor. But I don't feel that way. She's almost sixteen and should have a say-so. I also feel that the choice is the only power she holds over her illness. Lenny doesn't agree with me.

While Lenny and I are at this impasse, Melinda's losing ground. A decision needs to be made ... and soon!

MELINDA'S DIARY

June 7

Dr. Neely brought a woman named Jennifer to meet me today. She's twenty, but she had leukemia when she was eight and underwent a bone marrow transplant when she was twelve. Today, she is well and fine, goes to college and plays serious tennis. She really impressed me and after she was gone, I asked Dr. Neely if he thought a bone marrow transplant might work for me. He said, "It's a possibility."

I asked Mom and Dad about it and that's when I found out what's been going on between them. "You're fighting over what I should do?" I asked. "Don't you think I should be consulted?"

Dad told me about the clinic in Switzerland. I know exactly what each one of them wants me to do, but I told them I'll decide. I know they mean well, but I'm so mad at them for not talking to me sooner! It's my body.

June 8

Talked to Dr. Neely this morning and he explained how my immune system would have to be destroyed before the transplant—three days of radiation and ten days of chemo. The worst part is that I'll have to go into isolation! Ugh! I don't like that idea. But isolation will cut down on the risks of secondary infection, he says, which is very dangerous. Only medical staff and my parents can come see me, and everyone will have to be "de-germed" before they can come inside my room. He told me Mom will be my donor.

He also cautioned me that the transplant may take, or it may not. There are no guarantees that it will work, or that I really will be "cured" of leukemia. Most of the time, a BMT improves a recipient's life immensely and does produce a cure, but not always. This bothers me. To go through all this torture and have my cancer return would be the nastiest trick life could play on me. But if it works . . . well, I could dance again. I could be with Jesse.

Anyway, I've got lots to think about. I'll e-mail Jesse and talk to him about it.

TO: Ballerina Girl
Subject: Transplant

Just get well. I want to hang around with you for
the rest of my life.

Jesse

TO: Melinda
Subject: Transplant

Isolation? What's wrong with that? Can I join
you? Seriously, friend, I know it's a big decision,
but if the transplant works, then all this medical
stuff will be over. That will be a GOOD thing,
don't you think? Besides, if you go off to
Geneva, I'll never see you. Here, I might be able
to wave at you through a window!

Bailey

Elana's Journal

June 11

I talked with a woman today who had been a marrow donor for her brother. She told me what to expect from the procedure. I'll be under a general anesthetic and doctors will remove a pint or so of my marrow (which the doctor says I won't miss, because my body will step up production immediately to replenish my supply). They take it from my hip bones, and afterward I'll be sore, but back on my feet in no time. As soon as they harvest my marrow, they take it to Melinda for infusion. The downside is that I can't be with her during the infusion, because I'll still be in recovery. Lenny will hold her hand.

I asked Dr. Neely if there's anything I can do to make my marrow "better" for Melinda and he said, "No. You're not responsible for whether it takes or not, either. It either does or it doesn't."

Can I accept knowing my marrow didn't work if it doesn't take? That would be very hard for me. Knowing her chances are lowered because I'm not a "perfect" match is also hard. A sibling would be so much better, but Lenny and I could never have another baby after Melinda. We always wanted more children, but it never happened. Now Melinda's life is in jeopardy and a brother or sister would be such a blessing. Still, Dr. Neely assures me that unrelated donors help cancer victims all the time. I pray my marrow does the job for her.

TO: All Concerned
Subject: BMT

June 12, noon

Melinda's decided to go ahead with the transplant. Elana will be her donor and I'll be around to support both of them. I'd give anything to do more. In a few days Melinda will go into isolation, where they will begin giving her drugs to destroy her immune system. We're all scared silly.

Lenny

TO: Ballerina Girl
Subject: I'm coming!

June 13

Mom and I are coming to Atlanta BEFORE you begin the BMT process. When I came home from work last night, she gave me your dad's e-mail message and said she has a little money saved up and that she's going to spend it on the trip. She's reserved a room for us at a residence-type hotel that's near the hospital.

I hugged her big-time. I called my dad and told him I won't be coming this summer. When I explained about you, he offered to send us some money to go toward the trip. I was shocked. My parents haven't said two words to each other since the divorce, but now they're banding together to give me something I want more than anything else—a chance to see you up close and personal. One miracle down (my parents) and one to go (you getting well).

Jesse

TO: Jesse
Subject: Trip

Come as soon as you can! There's no time to spare.

MELINDA'S DIARY

June 13

Dr. Neely's not happy, because I want to wait a couple of days before he begins "killing" me—all right, maybe that's an overstatement. But I can't go into isolation until Jesse's here. Dad got Jesse's and his mother's fares comped by the airline, and they'll be here tomorrow afternoon.

Mom and Dad are throwing me a party here on the pedi-floor on Saturday. Besides Jesse and his mom, I've invited Bailey, Mrs. Houston, four girls from my dance class and three friends from school. Dad will videotape it and we'll have pizza, Cokes, ice cream and cake. I asked if I could have a pony brought up (ha-ha).

I'd love to spend some time alone with Jesse, but I can't figure out how or when. I'll think of something, because I WILL NOT go into isolation until the two of us can be together away from parents and nurses.

Dr. Neely showed me my "new" room. You get to it through an air lock, and anyone who's allowed to come in must wear a sterile gown, a hair covering and a mask. It's a bedroom with no decoration, but at least there's an intercom and a large window that looks out onto the hall, where people can stand, look in and talk to me. I can pull a curtain for privacy. It's kind of creepy knowing I have to stay inside the room while my immune system's down. I hope I don't go postal.

I'll have a TV to watch, but anything that comes in from the outside must be decontaminated. I'll be able to keep books and, of course, my diary, once all are "cleansed." I'm not looking forward to this one bit.

Elana's Journal

June 14

I can't believe the way Melinda looked when Jesse walked into her room. She fairly glowed! Ann looks wonderful too. She and I went down to the cafeteria to talk, but mostly to let the kids be alone together. Over coffee, Ann said, "They're in love, you know."

I said, "Yes, I know. Who'd have thought it would last so long. Ever since first grade!"

"He's never cared for another girl," Ann told me.

"I urged him to date others, but he wouldn't. He told me that Melinda was the only one for him and that someday they would be together."

I said, "I used to think that nothing would ever stand in the way of her dancing, but I forgot about love."

Ann said, "I've warned him about affecting her life plans for professional dancing. He said he'd stand beside her all the way."

"Cancer's in her way right now," I told Ann.

Ann reached over and patted my hand. "The transplant will change that," she said. "You'll have given your daughter life twice. Not many parents get that honor."

I'd never thought of it that way before, but it comforted me.

"I've missed you, Jesse."

"Same here. Can I hug you?"

"I'm not in isolation yet . . . hold me. Oh, Jesse, I'm scared."

"Me too. But I've read up on BMTs and there are plenty of success stories. Yours will be one too. When do you start?"

"I go into the Chamber, as I call it, on Sunday. Radiation starts Monday."

"Then we only have the rest of today and tomorrow to be together."

"That's right."

"We'll stay up all night. Can you do that?"

"Sure. The doctors and nurses are pretty understanding of my situation. Of course, they'll pop in to check on me occasionally, so we have to be on guard."

"How about your parents?"

"They know how hard this is going to be, so they won't hang around. Besides, I'll have plenty of time to sleep once I go into the Chamber. And Mom gave up her habit of sleeping here every night. But she gets here pretty early every morning."

"I just want to spend every minute I can with you."

"Me too."

"The party's a good idea. But is there any place we can go to be by ourselves?"

"I think so. I'll let Bailey help me work it out. She's clever and devious."

"I'll just bet. Know what I think?"

"I think you should kiss me before our mothers come back."

"You mean like this?"

Bailey's Diary

June 15

I know there are more blank pages in this book than there should be, but I forget about writing in it most nights. But not tonight. I need to "talk" to someone/ something. Seeing Jesse again and remembering the way I once felt about him was odd. Actually, I thought stirring up the old feelings would hurt more than it did. I never want Melinda to know how I've felt about Jesse. She's still the best friend I've ever had and I wouldn't hurt her for anything. The way I've felt about Jesse is my secret and I'll take it to my grave.

That said, I redeemed myself (in my own eyes) when I helped Melinda and Jesse be totally alone after the party.

I arrived in the afternoon, just before five, and the hospital offices were closing. I snooped the upper floors and found a lounge area with a couple of chairs and a sofa where I guess staff can relax. While staff people were leaving for the day and not paying attention to me, I pretended I belonged up there and unlocked the lounge door from the inside.

I showed up at the party (a good one too). Just a few people came. Melinda's dad showed a couple of videos: one of their European vacation (boring) and one of Melinda's dance career (much better). The clip of her and Jesse from the first grade really got to me. They were both so small and adorable. Even then, Jesse had the bluest, prettiest eyes. And Melinda was precious. I know more than ever that Jesse and I never could have worked out. He and Melinda belong together.

After the party, when everyone had gone home, Jesse and I helped Melinda sneak up the stairwell. She was wearing jeans, so she didn't look like an escapee, and we were lucky not to run into anybody climbing the stairs. The climb wasn't easy for Melinda, but we rested when she needed to, and with Jesse helping her, we got there without a problem. The floor was quiet; no one was around. I took them to the lounge. At the door, Melinda hugged me and said, "Thank you."

"How long have you got before you're missed?" I asked.

"An hour or so," she said. "I told a nurse on the floor that Jesse and I wanted to be alone for a little while and she said she'd save my room for last on eleven o'clock rounds."

"Thanks for helping," Jesse said.

My heart felt really tight in my chest, but I shoved the two of them inside, shut the door and dashed to the elevator. In the lobby, I met up with Patti, one of the girls from school who'd come to the party and who was driving me home.

She was miffed because I was so late. "Where've you been? You said you were just going to say goodbye and come right down."

I got teary-eyed. "Give me a break. It's not easy saying goodbye to your best friend. She's going to be locked up for weeks and weeks with the transplant and all. Maybe months."

Patti backed off.

Here I am alone in my room and all I can think of is Jesse and Melinda and how lucky they are to have each other. I have to stop writing now. I'm crying and the page is so blurry, I can hardly see it.

MELINDA'S DIARY

June 17, Morning

I'm in the Chamber, looking out my window at my world—a corridor in a hospital isolation care unit. They irradiated me from top to bottom (painless) to begin the immune shutdown sequence. Another dose tomorrow and the next day, then the chemo—the worst part.

I'll write about my evening with Jesse some other time, because I never want to forget a minute of it. We barely made it back in time for rounds, and we didn't sleep a wink, but our time together was perfect.

He tells me he'll be outside the window as much as he's allowed, and I told him to beat on the glass if I'm asleep, because I want to see his face as much as possible. We belong to each other. I understand now that I will never love anyone again the way I love Jesse. We are soul mates.

❧

June 23

Killing a person's immune system without killing the person is tricky stuff. The radiation left me sick, but it was nothing compared to what the chemo is doing. I didn't know I could be so ill and still be alive. Dr. Neely says it's normal—hope I'm spared abnormal. Everything else I've gone through seems like it happened in another lifetime. Except for Jesse. Seeing him at my window every day gives me the strength to endure. He presses his palm against the glass. I raise my hand and press my palm against his. The glass between us is hard and cold. But if I wait long enough, the glass warms slightly from the heat of his body. My body has no heat. I am cold all the time. I hold my hand against the glass for as long as I can stand up. And I imagine he is touching me. Really touching me.

June 25

The days are endless, the nights even longer. I asked Mom to hang a pair of my pointe shoes outside my window so I can see them. They dangle, all new and shiny pink satin and strong ribbon to wrap around the ankles. I want the shoes to remind me of

the world I left behind, of the life I long to have.
Ballet and Jesse, no cancer . . . this is what I want
more than anything else.

Elana's Journal

June 27

Today Melinda asked me to forgive her for "being
so crabby." I didn't know what she was talking
about, because she's always been the world's best
daughter. She said, "You and Dad are the best and
I'm so glad I got to be your child."

She scared me in a way because it was almost as
if she was saying goodbye.

TO: Our Closest Family Members
Subject: Update

I never imagined she would be so sick. I feel
helpless. And useless. I am a father without a
family. Elana hardly goes home, remaining at the
hospital day and night. We eat silently in the
cafeteria. I asked Elana to go out to dinner just

to get away for even a few hours. She refused. I've been abandoned by wife and daughter. Orphaned by this disease that consumes our lives. I'm not complaining, because this is just the way things must be right now. Yet I'm on the outside looking in, unable to help either of the two people I love most.

Lenny

Elana's Journal

June 27

Melinda reminded me that her friend Bailey's birthday is next week and asked if we would please see to it that Bailey gets a card. How can she think of others with what she's going through? Remarkable. Ann returned to California yesterday. Lenny and I agreed that we could not let Jesse leave with her. He'll stay until this is over or until late August, whichever comes first. He sleeps at the house in his old room, hangs at the hospital all day with me. He and Melinda touch by placing their

palms against the glass window. It breaks my
heart to see them stare into each other's eyes. Sometimes I wish the glass would dissolve, but then I remember, if it does, germs will invade and Melinda
has no way to fight.

TO: Jesse
Subject: Nightmares

I'm glad we can "talk" via Melinda's computer. I
want to hear every detail about her, but I can't
bear to go down and look at her every day like
you do. She's so thin and fragile-looking. Like she
might break and shatter. I keep last year's school
photo of her on my bedside table and I talk to her.
I tell her she's beautiful and smart and going to
get well. You are the glue that holds her together
now. I'm so glad she has you to love her.

Tell her that I've decided to transfer to tech high
school and get a diploma in design. I want to go
into the fashion business. I've been a crummy
student for years, but Melinda's commitment to
ballet has inspired me. Plus, she often looked at
my dress doodles and said, "Bailey, you should

design clothing. You're so good at it." I'll never have another friend like her. Please tell her that for me, Jesse!

━━━━━━━━━━━━━━━━━━━━━━━━━━━━━━

Elana's Journal

July 7

Melinda's feverish. Despite all precautions, she has become sick! We can't believe it. Dr. Neely is throwing massive doses of antibiotics into her, hoping to subdue any illness before it gets a toehold.

July 9

No change. Lenny and I sit by her bedside. Jesse waits at the window.

July 11

Viral meningitis! How could this have happened? We were all so careful. Dr. Neely says her weakened immune system has left her vulnerable. We watch our child waste away. We go nowhere, do nothing except stay by her side. She asked us to give Zorita to Bailey. I said, "No, Zorita's ours. She'll be waiting for you when you come home."

July 12

Melinda lies on the bed without moving, tubes running in and out of her. Antibiotics pour into her. Monitors and constant checks reveal no progress.

July 13

Lenny and I hold on to each other's hands and talk to her. The nurse said hearing is one of the senses that still works despite comas. Did I just write that? She's slipping away from us right before our eyes. Oh, God...how can this be happening?

July 14

Dr. Neely let Jesse dress in a sterile gown and come into the room. Jesse took her hand, kissed her palm and stroked her face. He spoke not a word, but I saw tears sliding down his cheeks. I put my arms around him and together we cried over Melinda and told her how much we love her.

July 14

I'm writing this because you can't. You're really sick, and all of us are scared. Your eyes fluttered open once yesterday and my heart jumped for joy. For a minute, I thought you were looking inside me. You looked as if you were saying "I'm sorry." As if you were apologizing because you haven't the strength left to fight. I begged you not to give up. But your eyes closed and you drifted away.

Where are you, Melinda? Are you safe and warm? Do you know we're here, on the other side of your consciousness? Come back to us . . . to me. Please don't leave.

Jesse

Received emergency call at 11:10 A.M. from ICU nurse who witnessed a seizure in this 15 y/o leukemic patient with recently diagnosed meningitis. Upon my arrival, patient was unresponsive and hypotensive. Blood pressure continued to drop despite rapid infusion of IV dopamine. Respiratory arrest ensued at 11:21 A.M. shortly followed by asystole on cardiac monitor. CPR was begun and patient was intubated. She received multiple doses of epinephrine and atropine. She briefly regained a pulse after 10 minutes of resuscitation, but went into ventricular tachycardia. Sinus rhythm could not be restored with IV lidocaine, and multiple shocks were administered via defibrillator. She remained in cardiac arrest. CPR was continued for more than 30 minutes to no avail. The patient never regained a heartbeat and was pronounced dead at 11:58 A.M. I met with family members standing by in the ICU waiting room and notified them of unsuccessful resuscitation efforts. Body will be taken to hospital morgue pending funeral arrangements by the parents. Submitted: 12:15 P.M., July 16

———————— ∿ ————————

Dear Mom and Dad,

I'm writing this the night before I go into the Chamber. I gave it to Bailey to put with my special box in my closet, because I know that you'll find it someday. Maybe next week, or even years from now when I've moved away and you've decided to clean out my room, but whenever you find it, I want you to know how much you both mean to me.

I know the procedure is a gamble. If it works, I'll be the happiest person in the world. If it doesn't . . . well, at least I didn't go down without a fight. Remember that. I wanted this chance. Mom, thank you for your bone marrow. Thank you for staying by me day and night (even when I was thirteen and not so very nice to you. I didn't mean to be hateful). I was so angry about having leukemia! Why me? Why did I have to get sick? I had so many plans. I was going to be a prima ballerina. I was going to dance all over the world. Instead, I was sick, on chemo, bald and hideous-looking. Dad, thank you for taking us to Europe. Thank you for letting me pursue my ballerina dreams.

This time around, I know that it's not all about ME. It's about making the best of whatever time I'm given. And about family and friends and leaving them good memories.

Thank you for being the two best parents in the

world. I've always felt sorry for Bailey and Jesse because they never had the kind of family I have. Not their fault either. It's simply the way life worked out for them.

Cancer isn't the worst thing that can happen to a person. And neither is dying young. Taking life for granted, living badly—these things seem far worse to me. In many ways—ways that count—I'm the luckiest girl in the world. Here's something I wrote when I was thirteen.

The Things I've Learned from Having Cancer

by Melinda Skye

1. Be GLAD for every new day.
2. It's okay to cry.
3. It's okay to feel sorry for yourself (but not too sorry).
4. Good friends are good medicine.
5. Love is the best medicine of all.

I love you both with all my heart. And I always will.

Melinda, your loving daughter

Elana's Journal

July 17, midnight

I went into Melinda's room and found her memory box on her closet shelf. On top was a letter addressed to me and Lenny. I held it for a long time before I found the courage to open it. The letter comforted me greatly when I read it. After Lenny reads it, I will make a copy and put the original into our safe-deposit box. It will be the thing I treasure most now that she's gone. Passages are already branded into my heart.

Her box held so many keepsakes important to her. I found a sealed letter with Jesse's name on it. I wanted to tear it open and read it, but I knew I couldn't betray her that way. I'll give it to him in the morning...the day of her funeral.

I found her first pair of ballet shoes from when she was five. Were my daughter's feet ever that small? I held them to my nose and could still smell the baby powder she used before she put them on. I cried so hard, I stained the satin.

Dearest Jesse,

If you're reading this, I didn't make it through the whole bone marrow transplant thing. You see, I wrote this letter before I went into isolation, and I gave it to Bailey to put in my memory box where Mom would find it and give it to you . . . just in case. I want you to know how sorry I am life didn't work out for us. We've grown up together, but we won't grow old together. Too bad. I'd have liked to see you become a doctor.

I found a piece of paper in my memory box with the class rules from the first day of school. I can't even remember why I kept it, but I did. The last rule was the best: Be kind to each other. Jesse, you have always been kind to me. I'm not sure why. I'm very ordinary . . . just a regular girl with a few dreams and some bad luck (leukemia . . . go figure). Here's something you should know: Having you in my life made me very happy. And that matters a lot when I had to cram a whole lifetime into just fifteen years.

Please don't miss me too much. Please don't be too sad. Find someone else to love, because you have much love to give and it's a gift that shouldn't be wasted. You, Jesse, were the rose that made my life sweet.

I will wait for you in heaven.

Melinda Skye

TO: Bailey
Subject: A Favor

I want to leave one final message with Melinda. I want to slide it under her hand in her casket, and I don't want anyone to find it and take it away. I want it to be with her for all time. If you can distract anyone who's standing by her casket when I come up for a final goodbye, I'd be grateful. Will you help?

Jesse

TO: Jesse
Subject: Re: A Favor

Yes. I'll help.

Bailey

It may be a lifetime before I see you again on the far side of time. Wait for me. Look for me. Please don't forget me, Melinda Skye, because one day I will come to you. I will come.

Jesse Rose